THE ECHOES OF SIN

JACK STEEN

ECHOES OF SIN

The unforgivable sin. An ex-minister. A created savior. The war between heaven and hell has begun...

With a past shrouded in secrets and a future hidden in lies, a supernatural force awakes within the small town of Redemption that threatens to undo even creation itself.

Once a minister, now a man lost in his faith, the last thing Nathan Hanlin wants is to be embroiled in a supernatural war that has nothing to do with him.

Or does it?

Being called the Protector of the human race is too unreal, and finding out he's half-angel/demon only makes things more insane. So when his whole world collapses, Nathan does the only thing he can do...he runs.

Except, there are supernatural beings on his trail, so there's nowhere he can hide, especially in a town like Redemption, which no longer feels like home for him.

Redemption used to be a sleepy town with one stop sign and one diner, and now it's the center of a war between the Guardians and the Protectors, and at its core is Nathan and he's tasked with undoing a mistake someone else made before time began.

THANK YOU

A huge shoutout to my VIP ADDICTS Subscription group.

If it weren't for you - I wouldn't have published this particular book. I know it's different but you embraced it and I appreciated it!

So here's a shout-out to those who are in the Ward and the Addicts tiers, but especially to the following for your constant encouragement:

Jan, Kerrihend91, Jen B, Snowgirl1638

If you want to become an Asylum Addict, join my VIP ADDICTS SUBSCRIPTION GROUP, where you'll get to read whatever I write for free and before anyone else and even get some free stuff. https://reamstories.com/jacksteen

Click to check it out...no pressure, but if you do sign up, be sure to say hello in one of the posts, and I'll raise a toast to you at the pub.

NOTE FROM JACK

If you are a fan of my Asylum Confession series - this is a book that is somewhat 'different'. I'm going to call this one a Jack Original.

I wrote it years ago and I've tinkered with it over time. I've always had a fascination with the idea of the Nephalim and the decision angels made to become better than God himself. Why is there an unforgivable sin for them and not for us, human kind? I don't have any answers, but I did have fun writing this story.

I originally uploaded this to my VIP Addicts Subscription group and they convinced me to publish this for you to read.

There are bad guys in this book.

There are some good ones, too.

There are demons and freaky happenings and things like Nephalim and torture and stuff.

Read and enjoy it for what it is - a way for you to escape for a few hours.

Enjoy the read.

CHAPTER 1
PROLOGUE

HE STOOD motionless in the cold, sparse room, visions of what was to come played out in his mind.

It was perfect.

Fresh rat droppings, along with the stench of mold, urine, and sulphur, filled the air. The aroma aroused him.

He rubbed his hands together as he viewed this small piece of paradise. The scorched cement blocks were a nice addition. The fingers of long-ago flames licked the walls and left burn patterns snaking toward the ceiling. The little cracks in the floor crisscrossed each other until the kaleidoscope of weeds peeping through the cracks decorated the floor. Ants and other insects scurried away from his boots as he walked around the room.

Chains anchored to the walls promised torturous delight. Exactly what his guest deserved. Saliva pooled and dripped from his lips as he imagined the hell he was about to create for her.

It was all for her.

Innocent. Humble.

A gift. For him.

PART ONE
THE RESTORER

NATHAN HANLIN

CHAPTER
TWO

NATHAN

It was time to say goodbye.

Nathan laid his hand on the frigid tombstone and closed his eyes. The usual platitudes of prayer wouldn't be welcomed. Not today. Not from him. She deserved more, even in death.

He'd known this day was coming, that he would need to step away from everything that held him back. The man he used to be was no more. It was time to stop pretending there was even a glimmer of hope left.

"I'm sorry Sue." The grief of the loss threatened to bury him. "I tried."

SUE HANLIN.
LOVED BEYOND TIME. TAKEN TOO SOON.

Nathan traced the words on the tombstone before he rose and dusted grass off his jeans. The moon cast an eerie glow throughout the cemetery, illuminating the tombstones around him. The silhouette of a bird perched atop an old stone cross was soon covered by mist as it rolled in off the lake.

During the day, the cemetery was a serene setting sitting on the shore of Redemption Lake. But now, this time of night, nothing was peaceful about the atmosphere. He shivered as a cool breeze whisked around him.

"Once upon a time was never enough. Not for us. Not for our love." Nathan looked one last time at the tombstone before turning away.

Once upon a time was meant for fairy tales, where true love conquered evil with a single kiss and a worthy prince slayed the dragon.

Once upon a time, Nathan had been that prince.

Now, he was the dragon.

CHAPTER
THREE

ROTTING CARCASSES LITTERED THE HIGHWAY.

Nathan Hanlin entered the twilight zone as he drove along the curving mountain road towards home from the cemetery. The remnants of ominous music played in his mind. If he didn't know better, from the dark swelling clouds filling his rearview mirrors to the dust swirls up ahead, Nathan would think he'd entered his own private hell instead of just leaving it.

Sentries of large black crows faced him on either side of the highway.

His recent nightmare come true.

For the past week his dreams were full of the reviling birds circling over a car wreck. Nathan shuddered at the memory. Crows were once used as messengers from the spirits, but if they were trying to tell him something, he sure as hell didn't want to hear it.

He rolled his shoulders, a weak attempt to ease a knot that had set in more than an hour ago. The highway lead toward Redemption, the small town he called home. Tonight, it stretched on forever. A chill had permeated his body hours ago. No amount of heat blasting from the vents could warm him up.

One day the icy tendrils of death would leave him. One day. But not today. Never today.

A horn blared behind him. A blur of black whizzed by, but he would recognize the bike anywhere. Eva Sine owned the only bike in the small town Redemption.

"Crazy woman." Her headlights danced their way across the darkened road as she maneuvered through the carcasses without a care.

Any normal woman would have slowed down the moment the first dead animal appeared. Not Eva. Everything was a challenge to her.

Even him.

Swerving to miss another unrecognizable pelt, Nathan's grip tightened on the steering wheel. The crows' beady eyes followed him as he drove past. It was unreal how they perched there, their black wings tucked tight against their slick bodies. Only their eyes moved, tracking him, stalking him.

He could have sworn they were looking directly at him. Not his vehicle. Him. As if they knew him.

The large bronzed archway leading to Redemption approached in the distance. Nathan pushed his foot until the speedometer inched higher.

Thirty feet ahead a barricade of large black crows were positioned beneath the large metal sign. Swirling clouds of dust sheathed the birds' movements, an illusion of a huge black dust storm. Hundreds of eyes stared at him.

You need us.

Nathan jerked his foot off the pedal. What the...?

He must have been more tired than he thought, which is not a good thing to be while driving on this road. His vehicle inched its way along, coming to a full stop right before the crows as their deafening caws filled the air.

The side windows and windshield cracked as the multitude of crows flew at him, their screams filling the air. Nathan ducked his head to his steering wheel, hands over his ears.

The glass shook from the impact.

Nathan's skin rippled from the onslaught of the invisible beaks poking at his skin. Fingers of dread funneled through his brain.

He cried out in anguish, begging God for help.

He jammed his foot on the gas, head barely raised above the steering wheel, and accelerated until he was past the swirling cascade.

Nathan gasped and struggled to regulate his breathing, each attempt a fail. Once beneath the archway, he glanced in his rearview mirror. He half expected to see the mass follow him.

Nothing.

No crows, no swirl dust, nothing.

The chaos had vanished.

He hit the brakes, his toes cramping from the quick movement. He leaned forward, arms resting on the steering wheel. Scratch marks ran along the hood. Nicked, dented, and littered with stray feathers, his truck looked like it had been dragged into hell.

Nathan went to reach for the door handle. His arms collapsed and chafed against the leather edge of the wheel before they fell onto his legs. His body shook as if an earthquake erupted beneath his feet, and there was nothing he could do to stop it. Pools of sweat poured down his face as they mingled with his tears.

What. The. Hell. Just. Happened?

CHAPTER
FOUR

JOANNE

She, who could see all natural and supernatural, was blind.

Joanne arched her body in an attempt to relieve the pressure of the unnatural twist to her wrists bound tight behind her bowed back. She cried out as she struggled to stand; her legs, frail and uncooperative, proved unable to support her aged body, and she crumpled to the floor.

A noise roared ahead of her. Her body shook with the vibrations that resonated through the cold wood floor. The air held the stench of sulfur that lingered and settled into the pores of her flesh.

Joanne gagged as the strength of the smell increased. An icy chill breeze teased her left cheek, and she twisted, desperate to escape the permeating odor, and gasped as a sharp object tore into her skin.

The heavy thud of a footstep sounded off to her right. One after another until they stopped.

Tremors shook her body as a hot, foul breath covered her.

Jagged claws clenched her face. A cry escaped through her lips.

Droplets of blood wound their way down her cheek, mixed in with her tears, and fell to her shoulder.

A horrific sound echoed through Joanne's mind.

Fear filled her veins.

"You are mine."

CHAPTER
FIVE

NATHAN

The streets were quiet as Nathan drove through town while his hands were still shaken from the recent attack. It didn't make sense. The time it took to reach Redemption from the Pass flew by in his desperate attempt to reach home.

When he first moved here to serve as Senior Pastor at Destiny Center, it reminded him of a town he'd seen in a Thomas Kinkade painting. Quaint and picturesque with white-picket fences, barking dogs, English gardens and the friendliest neighbors a person could ask for.

Central Park, in the middle of town, was dark. The lights on the walnut tree, lights that were always on, weren't.

The walnut tree, transplanted in the early 1900s, was an integral part of the town. During the summer, parties, and town meetings were hosted beneath its extended branches and thick trunk. Throughout the year, it would be lit up with white lights strewn throughout its limbs, which would shine for miles.

He'd even proposed under that tree.

The thing about the walnut tree is that the lights were never out.

Never.

It was a proud fact even displayed on a plaque in front of the tree.

The lights signified life, vitality, safety, and protection.

An urban legend asserted if the lights weren't ever on, their town would be destroyed.

Nathan never believed the legend until now.

Now, he wasn't sure what he believed anymore.

Nathan pulled into the parking lot outside of the small Second Chances cafe. When he'd first moved here, he couldn't get over the names of the streets, stores, and even the churches. Everything was tied back to Redemption.

Everything, since time began was tied back to the concept of redemption.

Despite the late hour, he hoped Jack, the owner of the cafe, or his feisty wife, Kate, would take pity on him and serve him a piece of the homemade apple crumb pie he knew would be waiting for him. Kate saved him a piece every night.

Or maybe Kate baked him a special cake. If anyone remembered, it'd be her. This year, he was okay if someone remembered.

When he pulled on the door, he was surprised to find it locked. He tapped on the glass with his knuckles and waited for Kate to lift her head from the counter she was wiping down. When she motioned with her hand for him to come in, he pulled on the handle again. With brows raised, Kate walked out from behind the counter.

"Are you just now getting back?" Kate held the door open for him.

Nathan nodded.

"You shouldn't stay there so long. Surrounding yourself with death won't help you live—" Her lips pursed at Nathan's glare, but she didn't finish her sentence.

It wasn't the first time she'd tried to talk to him about his visits to his wife's grave.

Kate was important to him, and he didn't like the dark circles beneath her eyes. He didn't even have to ask, he knew they were because of him.

Her unraveled silver hair escaped from her carefully coiled bun, and wisps of curly hair fluffed all over her head. The sound of her shuffled feet filled the diner as she grabbed a half-full pot of coffee.

Lukewarm and old was better than the sludge he made at home.

Nathan sat on one of the ripped red leather stools at the counter and glanced around. Three men remained in the store.

He nodded at Basil and the other man who sat with him in a booth nursing cups of coffee. Jack, Kate's husband, raised his cup as a salute to Nathan. The other man in the booth sat motionless with his head turned, looking out the window, not moving or making a sound.

Setting the cup of coffee down in front of him, Kate rested her elbows on the counter and gestured to the men.

"Well, Rev, we've got an old grump who won't go home," Kate said in a stage whisper. "Basil there has been playing with his cold cup of coffee for over an hour now."

"Coffee?" Nathan twisted his head to look at the old man. "Bay, are you sick?"

"Watch the dark. That's when they get you," Bay grumbled as he scooted out of the booth. He placed a bill on the counter and dragged his feet over to the door.

Ole' Bay mystified Nathan. He always had. He was a fixture of Redemption from the days of old, or so it seemed. Nathan didn't think he'd ever heard him utter anything sensible or even understandable.

Watch the dark? That's when who gets you?

Bay toward the door, gave him a slap on the back and he passed by and stumbled out the door. Drunk like usual.

Kate locked the door behind the old man. With drooping shoulders, she grabbed the last slice of apple pie for Nathan.

Rachel Gibbons, one of his best friends, made the best home-made pie around, and she always brought one into the diner around dinner time for him to enjoy.

They always met here, at the diner, instead of at each other's homes. A habit from his ministry days. Never be alone with a woman - friend or not. Always have witnesses around. Too many of his old friends had been caught in traps they couldn't get out of because they weren't careful.

Struggling not to let his disappointment show that the pie wasn't cake, Nathan patted the red vinyl stool beside him and waited for Kate to sit and rest her feet.

"I never thought Basil would leave," Kate sighed. "The old man came in over an hour ago and asked for a cup of coffee. Basil drinking coffee." Kate shook her head. "There was a time when he would only drink tea. If Jose was still around..." She pursed her lips. "You know he doesn't come in here very often anymore. Jack says it's cause I remind him of another time, another life. When he was happy." Her weary smile carries a hint of sadness. "Now, he'd rather nurse his JD over at the Powder Horn Saloon."

Nathan glanced over his shoulder and stared at the lone man left in the booth. Something about the man didn't sit right with him. He seemed too still and out of place.

"Are you waiting for someone to come by?" Kate nudged his shoulder.

"No, but who's the guy in the booth? How long has he been there?" Nathan said out of the corner of his mouth.

"What man?"

"In the booth, he's been staring out that window since I arrived," Nathan said.

"Rev, I think maybe you've had too much coffee for the night. There's no man sitting anywhere in this diner, except the one beside me asking me silly questions. Why don't you head off home and get some sleep since you obviously need it? That booth is empty."

He's not seeing things, is he?

Nathan pushed himself off the stool and faced the booth where there was a man, regardless of what Kate said.

A distance of six feet was between him and the stranger. With each step he took, a numbing sensation worked its way up his legs, tingling, until he could barely lift the dead weight of his feet off the ground.

Nathan strained against the effort, physically lifting his legs by sheer will until he reached the booth.

He looked for identifying features, trying to place the man, sure he'd seen him before. But his eyes wouldn't focus on any one spot. The more he stared, the more difficult it became. It was as if he was looking out through a train window, speeding by buildings that bled together the harder he looked.

Nathan scrunched his eyes, hoping to clear them, but all they did was sting. He forced them open.

Two steps away, Nathan leaned forward and placed his hands down. A wave of exhaustion and incredible sadness overwhelmed him the moment he touched the table.

The man's head twisted, and his black eyes narrowed as his focus turned from the window. Immobile, Nathan fought to breathe while a black haze floated across his vision. He stared deep into the man's gaze until he lost himself in the pool of darkness.

Indescribable horrors flashed through his mind.

Images of lightning, fire, and wings played for him. A child's cry. A woman's scream.

Nathan shook his head. The grip of fear diminished as he turned away from the man in the booth. The physical effects vanished with each breath he took. His feet no longer cemented, Nathan whipped around, only to find the object of his inspection no longer there.

Nathan searched the diner, hoping to catch a glimpse of the

man. Confusion overwhelmed him. Was he losing his mind? Oh God, he hoped not. Not now. Not like--

"Nathan, come on now, honey. You just come with me." Kate grabbed onto his hand and led him to the front door.

"I'm crazy, just like her," Nathan muttered as his head throbbed.

"I doubt that. I think your mind is usually quite clear."

"I swear there was a man inside your diner. When I looked into his eyes, I saw hell. Literally. And earlier, I was attacked by a demonic swarm of crows."

"Nathan, honey, I think you need to go home and get some sleep. You look exhausted." Kate left him at the front door and ambled over to the small kitchen sink hidden underneath the counter, placing Nathan's dirty dish and cup in there.

"Kate, my mind isn't playing tricks."

"Honey, you're tired. You keep runnin', too afraid to face your inner demons," Kate waved her hand at him. "Don't look so surprised. You're not that good of an actor. You rarely go home at night, instead, holing up in your office where you think no one notices. Go. Home." She pointed to the door. "You don't have to face those demons tonight, but you do need to sleep on something other than your office couch."

How did she know? He'd never told a single soul the truth about what had happened.

"Promise me you'll go home and get some sleep?" She patted Nathan on the cheek as he stood there puzzled.

He backed away as plumes of black smoke jetted out of the exhaust when she turned the key. It was time to either park this old piece of junk out in the field or fix it.

Maybe he'd talk Jack into donating it to the high school shop class.

Nathan hoped Kate noticed he didn't make any promises to her. He wouldn't do that to her, especially when he knew he wouldn't be keeping them. Going home in the evenings wasn't an option Nathan usually considered. Tonight, though, might be an exception.

Demons from his past couldn't be any worse than the ones he'd already faced tonight.

He'd grown up with a crazy mother who saw spirits in every corner. She always told him he had the gift, something he vehemently denied. Why would he be proud of a gift that destroyed his mother?

No. Nothing could be worse than what he'd already experienced.

CHAPTER
SIX

JOANNE

Drip. Drip. Drip.

Joanne's parched mouth ached as the water echoed against the metal it hit over in the corner. Her tongue swelled with each drip until the dryness of her mouth became unbearable. Afraid to make a sound, she lay on the cement floor, quivering with cold and dread.

She was caught in a nightmare. One of her own making.

She'd known for years that this day could come. Would come. But as the years passed, the threat of discovery, of remembrance disappeared.

She thought she'd been safe. She'd never been more wrong in her life.

Footsteps skulked closer. She counted the seconds it took for each thud on the floor. One foot lagged behind at a slower rate. She tried to figure out who her captor was, but she couldn't recall anyone with a limp leg.

Joanne trembled as the air filled with the stench of the

monster. Something inside of her warned her to get ready. She relaxed her body a second before flying through the air and being thrust violently against the wall. She couldn't breathe. Curled into a ball, her body ached as waves of pain tore through her. She couldn't contain the cries as she was kicked over and over. Joanne begged for the horrific beating to stop, but with her every mournful cry, the feral attacks increased.

She was going to die.

"You're not going to die. I have plans for you. I've always had plans for you." Cold hands gripped her face.

Joanne recognized that voice and knew.

He'd come back for her.

Every bone felt broken, every muscle torn, a trickle of blood welled up through open cuts, and pinpricks of pain danced along her skin. She prayed for darkness to overtake her, to consume her, and end her misery.

"Not only for you, Joanne, dear." Tremors flowed through her body as the voice hissed her name. Once upon a time, the demon had whispered her name like a silk caress against her skin.

Once upon a time when he'd been an angel in disguise.

The crackle of laughter filled the air. She'd forgotten he could read her thoughts.

"I've never been in disguise. You've always seen me as I am. As I should be. As I will be once again - thanks to you."

Joanne shook her head and ignored the pain. It wasn't possible. How could he know?

"You thought you could hide our son away from me? There is no place you can run that I can't follow. You thought your prayers to God would save you, didn't you?" The hatred and arrogance in the voice of the one she once used to love shook her to the core.

"You're mine, Joanne. The moment you pledged yourself to me, I stole your soul."

Darkness stole over her as she struggled to understand what he was saying to her. How could he steal her soul? How did he find out about her secret?

"Nathan," she whispered before she gave in to the bliss of darkness that surrounded her.

CHAPTER
SEVEN

NATHAN

Going home to an empty house really didn't hold much appeal.

As Nathan made a right turn on Grace Street, his headlights barely dented against the darkened road. It was as if a black shroud enveloped the street.

He cranked his neck to look up at the old-fashioned street lamps that normally illuminated the dozen or so aged Victorian houses.

They were all burned out.

Even his porch light was dark. Nathan glanced at the clock on his console. The timer wouldn't have gone off yet. He kept his porch light on till midnight.

He pulled into his driveway and killed the ignition. His neglected home didn't hold the warm feelings it once did. There was no laughter, no light in this building. What once was a home was now a house, and Nathan hated it.

He blamed God.

Nathan dragged his weary body out of the truck.

"It's about time you dragged your sorry ass home."

Nathan's blood stirred at the sound of the husky yet very sexy voice. He straightened before searching for the voice. The sharp squeak of the porch swing had him twisting his head before he caught sight of the one woman who tempted him to sin with every thought.

"How long have you been waiting?" He crossed the yard and bounded up the stairs. Suddenly he didn't feel as tired. The sight of her took his breath away every time. He'd never met another woman like her.

"All my life, darlin', all my life." Eva winked as she scooted down the seat, leaving room for Nathan to join her. She wore her signature black leather jacket with a red scarf wrapped around her slender neck. Her black hair was pulled up into a ponytail and swung to the gentle rocking of the swing.

"You say that every time," Nathan struggled not to jump when his leg hit hers. He casually readjusted himself so that only an inch separated them on the swing.

This woman made his blood boil in more ways than one. She was the bane of his existence, yet he needed her like he needed air to breathe, and it bothered him. Not even Sue had affected him this way.

"Maybe one day you'll realize I'm telling you the truth," Eva whispered before she bent down, reached between her legs, and pulled out a brown paper bag. "Here, I got this for you." She held it out.

Nathan shook his head. "I don't drink. You know that."

Shoving the bag into his hands, Eva swore. "It's not alcohol, you jerk." She pushed herself to her feet and stormed off his porch.

The sudden burst of anger surprised him. Going after her would do no good, so Nathan held the bag in his hands and just watched her leave. The tight jeans she wore hid little, and he'd be a liar to say he minded.

She jumped onto her motorcycle, pulled her helmet over her

head, and drove away, the squeal of the tires loud in the night air. He glanced at his watch. She'd be back.

She always came back.

Nathan sighed, sank back against the wood supporting his back, and glanced at the bag in his hands. Some days he didn't understand that woman.

She'd shown up in town a little over a year ago, standing out in her black leather pants, jacket, and boots. The first time he'd seen her was at the cemetery. The second was when he stood at the edge of the cliff far from town and looked down at the crystal clear waters of Redemption Lake, wondering why he shouldn't jump.

If it hadn't been for the sound of her motorcycle down a forgotten dirt road, he would have.

Ever since then, she'd always been there for him. At his darkest moments. When he felt most alone. Or troubled.

Nathan rubbed his hand over his face. He wanted a do-over. He deserved a do-over after the day he'd had.

Happy birthday to me. Not even Kate had remembered.

He slowly pushed his body off the swing and straightened. The brown bag slipped from his grasp and landed with a thud on the deck. He bent down to pick it up, but the bag ripped in his hands. A brown leather book slid out.

Kneeling, Nathan picked up the book and gently stroked the material. Soft. Like butter beneath his fingers. He opened the book and found blank pages inside.

A journal.

She bought him a journal.

A sharp pain sliced through his heart before he stood and walked down the porch steps.

Out of everyone in his life, why did it have to be her that remembered his birthday? Did she understand the significance of her gift? Probably no.

His footsteps heavy, Nathan headed towards his side

kitchen door. No one used the front door anymore. His foot nudged something he couldn't make out in the darkness.

Shadows lengthened across his driveway as he made his way to the door. The full moon illuminated the pathway for him, which was odd since the outdoor light should have been on.

Actually, the lights in the house should have been on as well. Yet the interior of his home remained dark.

Nathan laid his fingers on the doorknob, but before he could twist, it pushed open on its own. Cold fingers of dread tiptoed up his spine.

The door should have been locked.

CHAPTER
EIGHT

INSIDE, Nathan hesitated.

A heavy curtain of silence filled the house.

He hated dark houses. Hated dark corners. Hated anything dark. A light was always kept on. Always.

He flipped the light switch on and off, hoping for a miracle. The deafening stillness stretched until icy-cold fingers settled around his neck to choke him. Mentally shaking himself, Nathan tossed the journal in his hand onto the counter beside him and stiffened his back. Time to man up.

First, he needed music. And light.

The first thing he'd done after his wife, Sue, died was to hardwire the house with speakers in every room. Too many ghosts haunted him in the stillness, too many memories of a happier life taunted Saloon him.

He headed towards the pantry and fumbled around in the shelves until he found his flashlight. He grabbed his battery radio, matches, and his box of emergency candles. He set the radio on the kitchen table, turned the volume up loud enough to drown out his thoughts, and shone the beam of light into corners.

A bright flash caught his attention.

He inched his way towards his kitchen table, the light illuminating his path. His eyes were playing tricks on him. They had to be. Why else would a birthday cake with one candle be sitting in the middle of his table?

A card sat next to the cake. He stuck the flashlight in the crook of his arm and reached for the card.

Happy Birthday Nathan. May you find a sliver of happiness on this day meant to be celebrated. I promised no gifts, but everyone deserves a cake on their birthday. Love Rachel.

A vanilla coconut cake. He struggled not to smile, but it was hard. That would explain the opened door. She must have forgotten to close it properly. Maybe the lights had been out when she came and she thought she'd be helpful by leaving the door partially opened for him.

There was something about Rachel that tugged on his heart. She was delicate. Sensitive. Someone to be protected. His heart was too coarse. Too ugly. Blackening daily from guilt and anger. Yet, she pulled at him, creating a desire to be more than what he'd become.

She reminded him of Sue.

Nathan's shoulders sagged at the thought. Eva thought he was using Rachel as a replacement for his dead wife.

If only she knew.

Ignoring the cake, he made his way down the hallway, his feet scuffing along the hardwood floor. He set the flashlight down on the floor by his study, casting the shadow of his silhouette against the wall. His bedroom door was at the end of the hallway, where the light didn't reach.

To the right, his office door stood open. The moonlight shone through the open window, the curtain billowing as the night breeze whispered through the screen. His old worn couch beckoned. Maybe the midnight breeze would ward off any nightmares tonight.

He pulled the hand-knitted afghan across his body, and with his arm tucked behind his head, he surrendered to the weariness deep in his bones. A lonely keen from a mountain lion echoed through the night sky. Its eerie song drifted through the valley.

The heavy fog of Nathan's nightmare drew closer, the distant sound of a baby's cry echoed through his mind. A tear escaped through his lashes and slid silently down his cheek as he welcomed the sound, embracing it, knowing it would never draw closer.

CHAPTER
NINE

KATE

Kate stood at her front counter and evaluated the windows of her diner. They were covered in streaks her nephew missed. She grabbed old flyers and her spray bottle. Good help was hard to come by.

Breakfast aromas drifted out of the kitchen where her husband, Jack, slaved away at the stoves. Homemade grits, bacon and eggs, toast, and a strong coffee, were the morning staples at the cafe. In Redemption, most folks tended to congregate at the diner in the early morning before they headed to work.

This morning turned out to be quiet. Too quiet. Grumpy old Wilbert sat in his usual spot, complaining about the coffee. She never made it strong enough for him.

The conversation she'd had with Nathan last night replayed in her head. That boy was in a heap of trouble, and there was nothing she could do about it.

But she knew who could.

A tired smile crept over Kate's face as Rachel Gibbons

entered the diner, a swinging basket at her side. She was a breath of fresh air for Kate's weary soul.

"Jack, your favorite non-daughter is here! Make up some batter, will ya? Better make a double batch if you can," Kate called into the back.

"Come make it yourself, woman! Can't you see I'm busy?" His voice boomed.

Kate looked around the swinging door into the kitchen. "The only thing I see, old man, is you working on the crossword puzzle instead of making breakfast like you should!"

Kate turned in time to catch Rachel placing her hand on Wilbert's left shoulder. When she leaned over and gave him a peck on the cheek, Kate smiled. That girl's heart was as big as an ocean. Wilbert ducked his head, but Kate knew there was a grin on his face.

You couldn't help it around Rachel. Orphaned at a young age and raised by the local pastor, she was a woman who refused to let life interfere with her passions.

"Good morning," Rachel said before leaning down and placing a light, feathered kiss on Kate's cheek. She set the basket down on the counter and began to unfold the towels that covered whatever delicious treats she hid inside.

Kate's mouth watered. Rachel had recently rented out the little kitchen in the bakery next door. Jack considered Rachel a second daughter and refused to charge her whenever she came in for meals, so in exchange, Rachel would bake mouth-watering scones, muffins, and cookies for them to sell.

"Good morning, sweetheart. Jack is making some waffles, and I picked some strawberries from the field just for you." Kate said as she brought out the glass holders she kept just for Rachel's baking.

Rachel's smile lit up the room. "Hmm, fresh strawberries. Mind if I swing by later today and pick some more? I have a recipe for strawberry scones I'd love to try."

The little bell above the door jingled as Kate wiped her

hands on her apron. "Jack, Doug's here." Kate poked her head into the kitchen and eyed the pen that rolled off the crease in the crossword puzzle book.

"His order is ready." Jack motioned with his head to the side counter by the door as he poured batter into the waffle iron.

She blew him a kiss before grabbing the brown bag.

"If you happen to see Basil this morning, would you mind making sure he's all right? He was acting a bit strange last night," Kate walked down to the cash register and waited for Doug to join her.

"Strange? Bay?" Doug frowned as he pulled out his wallet.

"He was in here drinking coffee till closing."

"Basil?" Doug repeated.

Kate nodded. "Just make sure he's not getting sick. Tell him I'll have soup ready for him if he's in the mood."

She kept her eye on Doug as he left her diner. He never headed in the same direction when he left, yet she always assumed he went to meet Bay, wherever the old man could be found.

She poured coffee into two white mugs and handed one to Rachel, who walked towards the middle booth by the window.

"I wonder how Nathan's birthday went yesterday?" A sad smile crept onto Rachel's face as she cradled the mug in her hands.

"It took everything in me not to wish him a happy birthday," Kate sighed. "Nothing's gone right for that boy in a long time."

Rachel raised the cup to her lips. "I made him a cake." She gently blew the steam away before taking a sip.

Kate glanced up in surprise. "When I did that last year, he wouldn't speak to me for over a week. Are you sure that was wise?" The longer Nathan nursed his anger and hatred, the worse he became.

Tears welled up in Rachel's eyes. "I miss the man he used to be. I want to help him get back there."

Kate reached across and rubbed Rachel's cold hands. "Oh, honey. While I'm the first to believe in miracles, even that might be too much to pray for. Losing Sue and his baby the way he did on his birthday...I'm not sure he can come back from that."

Kate read the determination in Rachel's gaze. The girl had the heart of an angel, but Nathan--his wings had tarnished a long time ago.

"He can, Kate. Don't give up on him. Please?"

Shaking her head, Kate sipped her coffee while glancing around the cafe. Sure would be nice if it were busier. She could use a distraction. Even the main street was a virtual graveyard, with only Eva sitting in the park across the street. What was that girl doing all alone?

"What are you looking at?" Rachel asked.

Kate tore her gaze away from the empty streets. No sense in mentioning Eva, not now. Kate wasn't sure if it was jealousy or something deeper, but Rachel always froze when Eva was around. "There's something in the air...It's like a heavy shroud covered the town overnight. I didn't think there was a storm coming."

Rachel leaned back and set her mug on the table. "There's this old saying my father used to say. Every generation, evil takes form and steals the soul of the most devout."

Kate sighed. "There tends to be a kernel of truth in every tale you hear about our past. My grandma used to tell us kids stories about the evil one. How you could hear his lonely cry in the wind." She shrugged. "You tell me. Haven't you seen enough evil in your life?"

Emotions filtered across Rachel's face before she blurted out, "I'm scared that it's true."

Kate reached across the table for Rachel's hand and squeezed. "There's a scripture verse I try to remember when I get afraid. We are not ruled by a spirit of fear but of love, power, and a sound mind."

Rachel sighed. "Oh, I know, but living it is a different thing altogether. Do you know what I'm talking about?"

Kate pursed her lips. "I do," she said, "but don't allow fear to consume you."

"It takes a strong woman to face her fears and walk right past them. Sometimes I don't feel that strong."

"Oh, honey." It was everything Kate could do not to cry. "You are one of the strongest women I know." She thought about the hell Rachel had gone through as a young child. The horrors she'd had to face. "You've taught me a thing or two in my old age about embracing life."

Rachel's finger drew circles around the rim of the coffee cup. "At my real father's old cabin, there was a book he used to read whenever he was drunk. I think it was a journal he found from a miner. I remember him reading me the stories late at night. I'd get nightmares. He said I needed to learn to face my fears instead of indulging in fairy tales."

Kate leaned forward. It wasn't often Rachel would talk about her childhood. God knew they weren't full of good memories.

A drunken mother and an abusive father. Kate knew you should never speak ill of the dead, but Rachel's parents were no angels. "What's so special about this book?"

"I think it might have the answers we need. If this myth is true, this journal might hold the secret to saving the soul of the most devout." Rachel's face blanched as she whispered the words.

"Do want me to come with you?" She knew right away that Rachel intended to go to the cabin for this book. But as far as she knew, the girl had only ventured to the cabin twice in her life since her father killed her mother and left Rachel alone in the woods.

Rachel shook her head. "No. This is one fear I need to face. His ghost can't scare me. Not anymore."

Kate didn't think that was a wise move. "Take Nathan with you."

Rachel's brow lifted. "He's too scared to face his own past. I don't think asking him to face mine would be right. Not now, at least. Our relationship seems to be at a standstill." Rachel shrugged her shoulder. "I'll be fine."

Kate bit her lip. Jack would be telling her to mind her own business right about now.

"Do you love him?"

A myriad of emotions covered Rachel's face. "It's hard to love a man who won't be honest with you, let alone himself." She sighed. "It's even harder to love a man who doesn't love you back."

Kate shook her head. That wasn't true. "He loves you, Rachel. He's just confused. His anger towards God masks everything else in his life."

The smile Rachel gave Kate was half-hearted. "He doesn't seem to be confused when it comes to Eva. Have you noticed that?"

Kate had. And she didn't like it.

Kate sat in silence, contemplating her answer. She casually glanced back out the window and noticed Eva was no longer alone. Nathan now sat beside her on a park bench, facing the large walnut tree in the center.

Something was going on between those two. Since the day Eva first drove into town on that fancy motorbike of hers, she'd stuck to Nathan's side like glue.

Kate pursed her lips. She didn't like it. Not one bit. If that boy had any soul left to save, spending time with that devil's child wasn't the answer.

"Don't give up hope," Kate said. "He needs you. More than he knows."

CHAPTER
TEN

JOANNE

A chair scraped against the cold hard floor. Joanne struggled to raise herself up from where she lay.

"I've got to tell you, Joanne, for a while there, our son was turning out to be a disappointment."

"He's not your son. He'll never be." She spit the words out as her anger rose to the surface. She bit her lip. Letting him rile her was a mistake.

"There's the spunk I've missed."

Joanne snorted, then winced at the pain. "I doubt that." The moment he'd walked out of her life forty years ago proved it. So why was he back? There was nothing she could do for him.

"You're wrong. Why do you think I picked you in the first place? That wasn't a random meeting. I didn't set foot in a church to pray to God." The disgust in his voice mystified her. She'd forgotten he could read her thoughts.

"What do you want, Max? Or is that even your name?"

The chill in his laughter caused shivers to run along her skin.

"Close. Morax." The pride in his voice sickened her.

Morax. Dread filled her soul. The last name of her doctor was Morax.

How? She would have recognized him. Dr. Morax was a Christian man, she was sure of it. She never saw demons surrounding him. There was a bright glow about him. It's why she trusted him so much.

Then she remembered that she'd never seen demons around Max either. Not until the very end.

"What do you want?" She couldn't imagine what he wanted with her. It didn't make sense. She was older now, while he sounded as if he'd never aged.

She hadn't lived in the real world for years. Her son had forgotten about her. She was of no use to the man she'd once loved more than life.

"The pastor aspect to our son surprised me. Your influence was too strong. So was that weak-willed woman he married. I knew getting you out of the way was the key. He's right where I need him to be. And don't worry, he's not alone. Hasn't been for a long time. And soon he'll realize that."

She was glad for her forced blindness.

For years she'd longed for just one more look of his face but now she welcomed the dark. The cold from the cement seeped into her bones, and she tried to readjust her angle. Her numb limbs wouldn't respond.

At the snap of his fingers, icy talons grabbed hold of her body and lifted her. Demons. His minions. If she'd been able to see them when she'd first met Max, she would never have fallen for him. It wasn't until afterward after she'd given her virginity to him.

The radiant skin of a fallen angel only diminishes with time. It fades but never goes away.

"Leave me alone," she muttered, angry at herself for dwelling on him, on their past.

"I've never left you alone. Why would I start now?" The husky tone of Max's voice warned her.

Her body stiffened when he held her and drew her close. She angled her head away from his chest. She stifled a scream as it lodged in her throat. He took three steps and placed her on a softer surface. Rusted springs creaked as her weight bore down on them.

"I'm hurt, Joanne. To think that after all my tender care towards you as a patient, you would feel this way about me now. Have I ever let you down? I gave you the greatest gift I could. A son. Our son - made for greatness. I've taken care of you when everyone else forgot you. I'm hurt."

Her hands fisted, and her nails dug into her palms. Sincerity dripped from his voice like poison from a forked tongue. Under her breath, she prayed the Lord's Prayer.

"Why do you bother? He's already given up on you. He tested you, and you failed. He may be the God of second chances, but when you sell your soul to the Fallen, you gave up any right you had to his forgiveness."

She listened for his footsteps. She needed him to walk away. To leave her alone. To stop reading her every thought.

"I'll never leave you. Nor forsake you."

His bitter laugh as he walked away filled her with dread.

CHAPTER
ELEVEN

NATHAN

"Aren't you freezing?"

Nathan scuffed his feet against the fallen leaves. He hunched his shoulders against the brisk wind at his back.

Eva shrugged. "I feel alive. That's what matters, isn't it?" She patted the space beside her on the bench.

He glanced over his shoulder towards the windows of the cafe. He'd seen Kate in the window earlier, sitting with Rachel when he'd pulled up, but it was the draw of a motorcycle parked across the road that pulled him.

He cleared his throat as he sat down. "I owe you an apology."

"Yeah. You do." Eva crossed her arms.

She wasn't going to make this easy for him.

"Thank you for the journal. It's been a long time since I last wrote in one. I--"

"Need it. I know." A brief smile graced her face, her cheeks flushed from the cool breeze. Her long black hair rose slightly in the wind, and Nathan swallowed.

"How did you know?" He'd never told anyone about his journalling habit that died along with Sue.

Eva's eyebrow rose as she twisted towards him and rested her arm on the back of the bench. "It's kind of hard to miss your bookshelf full of journals. I noticed you didn't have one yet for this year or for last year. I know it'll be hard, but..." Her shoulder lifted in a shrug as she bit her lip.

"Sue used to buy me my journals." A shiver ran down his back. He'd promised Sue yesterday at her graveside that he'd start to journal again.

"She never would have wanted you to stop." Her fingers teased the back of his neck with their gentle caress. It didn't take much for him to imagine the feel of her fingers in his hair-- *stop*. He shouldn't be going there with his thoughts.

"There's a lot of things Sue wouldn't have wanted me to do that I've done since her death." Nathan shrugged.

Eva gave him a smile that told him she knew more than she let on. More than he thought she knew. "You're a changed man. Don't beat yourself up over what could have been. Living in the past only hurts you, no one else."

Silence reigned between them. Memories of decisions made played out in front of Nathan. Of stepping down as senior pastor, of turning his back on God. Decisions he could never redo. He glanced at Eva only to find her staring at him.

Eva nodded her head towards the cafe. "Go on. They're waiting for you."

Nathan glanced over his shoulder. The parking lot to the cafe was empty save for his Jeep and two pickup trucks, which was odd. The place was normally packed in the mornings. Everyone came for Jack's breakfast of waffles or eggs.

The sight of her motorbike snagged a memory.

"When you zipped past me yesterday on the highway, didn't you notice the crows?" They'd invaded his dreams last night, their beady eyes hounding him.

Her eyes darkened as she stared at him before turning her

head and staring off into the distance. "Yeah, I noticed." Something in her voice caught his attention.

"I've never seen so many of them before, not like that."

Eva withdrew her arm from the back of the bench and gripped her hands together. "My...father...believes the gods use them as messengers," her voice dropped.

Nathan leaned forward. Eva never talked about her father unless it was to call him the devil incarnate.

"He used to tell me if I ever needed help, to search for a crow. There would always be one around when I needed it." She laughed, bitterness laced in the sound. "What parent tells his daughter to search for a crow?" She shook her head.

Nathan noticed her knuckles were white.

"The funny thing was, he was right. Whether I want them there or not, there is always a crow." She bit her lip, the sadness evident on her face. "Never a father."

Nathan reached out and covered her hands with his own. Eva unclenched her hands and threaded her fingers through his. She winked as he smiled at her.

"Go on," she said. "If you're not careful, Kate will serve you cold coffee."

Nathan stood but didn't let go of Eva's hand. He didn't think he could even if he had wanted to. "Come with me."

Eva chuckled. "Kate would have a heart attack if I stepped foot in her store. And poor little Rachel would be beside herself. I don't mind sharing you." There was a gleam in her eyes, a predatory glance. "For now." Her smile faltered as she looked away.

Nathan took a step back, letting go of her hand. He watched as she clenched her fist and stuck both hands inside her black leather jacket pockets. She leaned back against the bench, kicked out her legs, and crossed them at the ankles. Her head dropped back, her black hair swinging close towards the ground. The way her lashes brushed her cheeks as she closed her eyes...Nathan's heart skipped a beat.

Mine.

The thought startled him. He turned towards the cafe, knowing there was another woman inside he should be claiming instead. If he had any hope of redeeming himself, of getting back to the life he once had lived, it was with Rachel. Not Eva.

So why was every step he took away from the beautiful woman on the bench difficult? Why did his throat tighten at the thought of leaving her?

A harsh caw filled the air. Nathan glanced up to find a single crow circling the air above him.

"See Nathan. They're always there." Eva's voice carried across the park.

CHAPTER
TWELVE

NATHAN RUBBED his chilled hands together as he stepped into the cafe. He spied Jack in the corner pouring coffee into mugs resting on a tray.

"Please tell me one of those is for me," Nathan called out as he walked over to where Jack stood.

The big man shrugged one shoulder before he turned, a fierce frown covering his face.

Nathan smiled sheepishly. He had no idea why Jack was in a sour mood, but he knew enough to keep quiet.

"About time you got here," Jack grumbled as he grabbed another mug and slammed it down on the counter. He glared at Nathan while he filled it up to the brim with coffee.

"Damn diner is too quiet this morning. Crazy folks believing demons walk the streets." Jack narrowed his gaze.

Nathan gave a quick glance over his shoulder to the empty street outside. "What demons?" He noticed Eva still sat on the bench, her body hunched over so that her hands hung below her knees. He never did ask why she was out there, alone.

Jack growled low under his breath, causing Nathan to take a step away from the counter. Pure anger filtered across Jack's face as he glared at Nathan.

"What's going on, Jack?"

"As if you don't know." Jack marched around the corner of the counter. Nathan took another step backward, but the back of his legs hit the bar stool.

"You need to ask?" Jack stabbed his finger against Nathan's chest. "You brought a demon into this diner last night."

Nathan's eyes widened. "It was already here." His chest ached. Jack had used every ounce of strength in his bulging muscles, and damn, it hurt.

"Whatever that ...thing...was, it was already here when I arrived," Nathan said, his voice insistent. "Kate served the man a coffee. I didn't bring him...it...in." Anger boiled inside Nathan's soul. How dare Jack accuse him of something like that.

Jack glanced behind him before directing his gaze back at Nathan. "Kate saw nothing. You were the one to see that cursed thing last night. Not Kate. Don't go blaming her for something that is your fault."

Nathan brought his arms up and knocked Jack's hand away. "I'm not blaming anybody for anything. What is your problem today?"

Jack took a step back before rubbing his hands over his face. When he took them away, he looked haggard.

"Something is happening in our town, and I don't like it. Not when it affects Kate. Cause then it affects me. You've got her worried, boy. You keep running in circles when it comes to the calling God has on your life. And let me tell you --I'm getting tired of seeing you make the same mistakes. Reminds me of my dog chasing its tail."

Nathan's jaw dropped. Jack was the one man Nathan knew would always be there for him, supporting him and offering a listening ear when Nathan needed it. Not once since before Sue's death had Jack confronted him like this.

"Well, Jack--"

"Don't bother trying to explain. I've had enough of all your

silly excuses and explanations. Mood swings are fine for children, but you are a grown man. When you're beaten down, act
like one. Swing back. There's always a season for sorrow and
questioning. I reckon God ain't too afraid of our questions, and
He'll even give us a bit of leeway when we need them. Yours
have gone on for long enough." Jack crossed his arms. "Step up
and be the man God made you to be instead of the boy you
used to be." He turned away and headed back to the kitchen.

"Now go on over and give my Kate a big hug. She's been
waiting for you." Jack called over his shoulder.

Nathan sat stunned, not sure how to react or even what
to say.

Sure, he was mad at God. Why wouldn't he be? God let his
wife and unborn child die.

Every man made a course change in their life at one time or
another. Just because he used to be a pastor didn't mean he
always had to be one. It didn't mean he wanted to be one,
either.

Why believe in a God who didn't believe in you?

CHAPTER
THIRTEEN

KATE

Kate couldn't figure out Jack this morning.

She heard the tongue-lashing he'd given Nathan. Everyone in the diner had heard. It'd been a long time coming, but that didn't excuse his gruffness.

The man was cranky and she hated to see Jack in that mood. She relied on him to be her rock, especially when she was having a bad day.

Like today.

"Sorry, Kate," Nathan mumbled as he sat in the booth beside Rachel and reached for her hand.

"What are you apologizing for?" She leaned back in the booth and watched the silent exchange that occurred between the two.

"You don't need to worry about me. I'm okay," Nathan shrugged his shoulder before reaching for his coffee mug.

Kate snorted. "That's the largest bald-faced lie I've heard today. Try again."

Nathan just shrugged. Kate shook her head at the boy.

Someday, he'd get rid of the blinders he wore. She just wished the walls he built around his heart would crumble. She was getting tired of the hard exterior.

"Was the cake okay?" Rachel's soft voice broke the silence.

Kate held her breath, unsure how Nathan would respond. If he hurt this girl, she'd make sure Jack broke a few fingers. Her lips pursed together. Son of her heart or not, the boy needed to learn a lesson if he broke Rachel's. She caught the brief clouding in his gaze as he glanced at her before looking towards Rachel.

"I ate half of it for breakfast. Thank you," he said.

The smile on Rachel's face warmed Kate's heart. The boy done good. Kate gave a small nod before hearing the slam of the kitchen door. She turned slightly to watch Jack wink at her as he came towards their table.

She shouldn't have doubted the boy. Rachel deserved to be treated like a queen, and she had no doubt Nathan was the man to do it, once he let go of his anger. Until then...Kate shook her head.

Everyone had their own personal journey to follow.

Jack laid out plates of freshly made waffles covered with strawberries on the table. For Rachel, Jack added some whipped cream on the side. He tended to indulge Rachel in her sweet tooth whenever he could. Kate gave Jack's hand a squeeze before he turned away.

"Honey, would you mind bringing over a fresh pot of coffee? I think we're going to need it. None of that decaf stuff you try to sneak on me, you hear?" Kate said.

Jack's eyes crinkled at the corners when he smiled at her.

She turned her attention to Nathan. She needed to know he could handle her next words. She'd minded her thoughts for a while now, waiting for the right moment. After Jack's lashing earlier, adding her own two cents wouldn't hurt. She just prayed he was ready for it.

"Honey, last night you plum scared me. I couldn't sleep all

night 'cause I was so worried. I think something's going on, and it's time you paid attention."

Nathan dropped his head onto his hands and sighed. Raking one hand through his hair, he glanced over at Rachel. "I am paying attention."

"Are you?" She knew there'd been a demon in the diner. What bothered her was that she didn't sense it. Her, of all people, should have.

So why had Nathan?

"I'm not blind. I know what I saw." Nathan leaned back and took a sip of his coffee. "I don't understand it. Why me? I'm a nobody. Certainly not a threat. So why would I be seeing demons and not you?" He pushed his coffee cup away. "Don't tell me God is trying to get my attention. He had it years ago, and He walked away from me, not the other way around."

Off to the side, a 'harrumph' sounded.

"What did I tell you earlier, boy?" Jack said. "You should be thanking those lucky stars of yours God hasn't given up on you yet. Instead of loving you the way He does and putting up with your foolishness, He should be giving you a good time out like the young parents today do. Why, in my day, you would have been taken out to the old woodshed--"

"It's a good thing your parents aren't around to hear you say this," Kate said, interrupting him. "Your parents didn't even have a woodshed, you old grump."

"Harrumph," Jack grunted as he turned away. The bell on the diner's front door jingled, alerting him to a new customer's arrival.

The three occupants of the booth sat in silence for a minute. Kate waited for Nathan to speak first. Rachel only bowed her head.

Nathan grabbed his coffee cup again, took a sip, and set the cup back down on the table with a thud. "I lost my wife and child. Where was God on that night? I've moved on. I can't forget what happened, but it's in the past. I'm ready to move forward with my life. Doesn't mean I have to ask God to hold my hand while I do it. I don't trust him. Not anymore. I don't think I ever will."

"Then I feel sorry for you," Rachel whispered. A sheen of unshed tears welled in her eyes, and an unrecognized anger welled up inside of Kate.

"You can't blame God for what happened to you. Those were man-made choices, not God-ordained ones." Kate clenched her fist as she struggled to keep her voice low and level.

Nathan shook his head. "There was no reason for Sue to veer off the road that night. She grew up in these mountains. I don't care what anyone says. She didn't just drive off the side of Crow Mountain. She was killed. God could have protected her. Where were her angels that night? They did nothing to protect her. Nothing."

Nathan pushed himself away from the table and stood. Kate reached her hand out to stop him, but before she could, something large hit the window, and Rachel screamed.

CHAPTER
FOURTEEN

NATHAN

A shudder ran through Nathan's body as he stood mesmerized at the window. He couldn't believe what he was looking at. Within a span of less than fifteen minutes, the world he'd known outside had changed. Drastically.

What had earlier been a grey, dismal type of day was now hell on earth.

The sky illuminated an eerie blood-red sun hidden behind midnight black clouds. Large, heavy clouds blew in over the mountains and hid the sun, casting a demonic glow.

Thump. Thud.

Dead crows fell from the sky, their lifeless bodies covering the street outside.

He glanced at the park and saw another body lying on the ground.

Eva!

Nathan bolted towards the front door only to be stopped by Jack, who stood in his way.

"Rachel needs you. There's nothing you can do for the dead birds."

Nathan glanced behind him. Kate had her arm around Rachel while they stared outside.

"She's fine. Eva is out in the park." He pushed at Jack, who refused to move. "Get out of my Jack. She needs help." He waited till Jack moved before he pushed on the door and stepped outside. "Call the ambulance," he called over his shoulder.

Nathan quickly glanced up into the sky. The crows were falling out of nowhere. What the hell? Sidestepping and praying to God he didn't get hit, Nathan raced across the street and over to where Eva lay on the ground, curled up into herself.

It took him a moment, but he realized that all around Eva, the grass was clear. Everywhere Nathan looked, dead birds littered the ground, but around Eva, there was nothing.

Kneeling down, he gathered Eva into his arms. "Are you okay?" She rolled her face towards his chest, her body heaving. A deep overwhelming need to care for her filled him. Fear stoked his heart as she sobbed in his arms. He didn't know what was wrong or who had hurt her, but he'd never seen Eva broken like this. Never.

"Tell him to stop." Eva gripped the collar of his jacket and raised herself up in his arms. He stared into her eyes, unable to look away. Her irises were so dark, he would have sworn they turned black.

"Tell who?"

"He has to stop. He's killing them for no reason," she sobbed. "It's my fault. It's all my fault." Eva released his collar and collapsed back in his arms.

Nathan gathered her close and rocked her. "Who, Eva?" He whispered against her hair.

A shudder ripped through her body. "M--"

"Nathan!" Rachel screamed his name, the sound reverberating through the park.

Nathan whipped his head around, his arms tightening their hold on Eva.

Rachel stood outside the cafe, her arm outstretched as if reaching for him, horror etched on her face as she screamed his name again.

Time stood still as Nathan turned to view where she was pointing. The large walnut tree located in the middle of the park had uprooted and teetered. A sudden gust of wind picked up and whipped around the tree, the leaves on the ground funneling into a cloud around where he sat. Nathan's body froze as he watched the tree tip toward where he sat on the ground with Eva.

Move! Nephilim, son of Morax, move!

Nathan's eyes widened as a dead crow rose from the ground, flapped its black wings, and hovered a foot away from where he sat.

The dead crow spoke to him. *The. Dead. Crow. Spoke.*

"Move, Nathan. We have to move." The weight in his arms struggled against his hold. He glanced down at the woman he'd briefly forgotten. Eva's face scrunched as she fought against him.

"Move, damn it. I'm not ready to die." She pushed her hands against his chest, forcing him to fall backward. His arms let go, and as he fell, Eva sprang to her feet. She reached down, grabbed his hand, and hauled him upwards.

They weren't going to make it. The crow uttered a sharp 'caw' before rising in the air. Eva yanked on his hand, forcing him to jump out of the way. A gust of wind shoved at his back, pushing him further than he thought possible. He landed with a thud on the grass, his breath knocked out of him.

"You idiot! Why did you stop?" Eva sat beside him, hunched over her knees, her hair windblown and filled with dry leaves.

Nathan rolled over to his side and raised himself up. His whole body felt bruised. He stared, amazed at the old walnut tree. It landed exactly where Nathan and Eva had sat, its branches broken and scattered all over the park. There was a large empty hole where the tree once stood.

"Eva. The crows..." Nathan stood and turned, searching the park and the main street for the black bodies. But there were none. None. All the crows had vanished.

Eva slowly stood to her feet, brushing off her jeans. "They're gone." Her eyes closed as a smile graced her face. She raised her face up to the sky and laughed. "I knew you couldn't kill them," she whispered.

Nathan took a step towards her. "Who are you talking to?" None of this made sense to him.

Biting her lip, Eva reached her hand out. Nathan took it, winding his fingers through hers. The warmth of her skin wove its way up through his arm and into his heart. Like always.

"Nathan, we need to--" Eva's eyes narrowed before she dropped his hand and stepped back.

Before he could remark on the closed look in her eyes, arms closed around his chest and squeezed. He glanced down at the small wrists wrapped around him. Rachel.

"I'm so glad you're okay," she mumbled behind his back as her head rested against him. He turned and wrapped his arms around her small frame. Her hair barely came up to his chin.

Nathan rested his chin on Rachel's head as he watched Eva back away. The wink she threw at him before tossing her hair threw him for a loop.

He wanted to let Rachel go and run after Eva, but something inside of him held him back. Something always held him back. He couldn't understand it. It was as if his heart belonged to two different women, no matter how hard he fought it.

Rachel needed to be loved.

She deserved to be protected and kept safe. Cherished. Her pure heart didn't deserve his blackened one, yet no matter how hard he tried to keep her at a distance, she was always there. Waiting.

She believed that there was more to him than there was. She

saw something in him that even he couldn't see. She believed in him. Or rather in who she thought he could be.

Eva, on the other hand, accepted who he had become and didn't try to change him. She understood his scars were too deep. She didn't try to push him to be someone he wasn't.

She didn't need him, but she wanted him. Or at least, he thought she did. She was one woman who got him so twisted he wasn't sure what he wanted or didn't want.

No one, not even Sue, had done that to him.

He rubbed his hand in a circular motion on Rachel's back as he watched Eva stride her motorcycle. He had no doubt he'd be seeing her again. He had some questions she needed to answer. A quick glance at the ground confirmed that.

CHAPTER
FIFTEEN

NATHAN WALKED through his empty house, thankful for the white noise of the radio in the background. After leaving Rachel in Kate and Jack's tender hands, he escaped the carnage of the park and drove for a long time down the back streets and mountain roads. He needed time to decompress, to understand what had happened.

Everyone there had seen the dead birds that littered the street and park. The dead crows weren't a figment of his imagination. So how could they just disappear?

Rachel said she'd seen them all fly away after the walnut tree had fallen. But how was that possible? Why didn't he notice? The ground had literally been a sea of black feathers one moment and clear the next.

They didn't fly away. They disappeared.

He didn't even want to think about the fact one had spoken to him. Nathan ran his fingers through his hair. He wasn't going crazy. He couldn't be.

He roamed through the house, unable to settle in one spot, and paused at the one door that had stayed closed since the day Sue died. He reached his hand out, but it faltered before falling down to his side. He bowed his head before bending forward and resting it against the wood.

His life had changed in one moment. He wished for the clock to turn back, for choices to be remade. He wished for the innocent belief he'd once held towards God.

That one awful moment held the power to change not only his life but also his faith.

Nathan stood that way before he exhaled and stepped backward. Every day he tried to open the door and to step inside. Every day, at the last moment, he wouldn't, couldn't, open the door. He wasn't ready yet to face those inner demons.

He headed towards his study and sat in his chair. Nathan loved his study. He picked up a book and reread the first page for the fourth time before setting the book down.

Kate said you couldn't turn back time, that you had learned to let go and 'let God.' But letting God do anything was pointless.

No matter how hard you believed, no matter how good of a life you lead, it didn't matter.

Rachel believes that things happen for a reason. But what reason does death hold? Jack said Sue's death was accidental. That it was no one's fault, but he was wrong.

It was God's fault. Nathan believed that with all his heart.

Sue knew the mountain roads like the back of her hand and would never speed through the windy trails. Especially being pregnant. Keeping their child safe was all that mattered to Sue. She would never purposefully kill herself and their child. Never.

He knew all the platitudes, all the right things to say. He used to be a pastor. Of course, he knew what scriptures to quote and what words to pray. Didn't mean they were real, or even true.

He would never admit God wasn't at fault. It should be God's fault. Nathan gave up everything for him. Sacrificed everything.

Nathan's hand fisted, and he punched down on the arm of his chair. He even sacrificed his mother, all in the name of God.

This time there was no sacrificial lamb to the rescue.

God could shout it from the rooftops. Send an angel to stop him in his tracks. Visit him face to face. Have bloody crows speak to him. Didn't matter.

Demons or not, folklore be damned, Nathan didn't want to hear God's reasonings.

CHAPTER
SIXTEEN

NATHAN PERUSED the books on his shelves. Maybe now was the time to get rid of some of the stuff he would never use again. His Biblical Thesaurus, Greek translations, and references weren't for everyday life. Jim, the interim pastor they brought in to cover Nathan's absence after he stepped down, could probably use them.

On the top shelf were some old books he'd inherited from the previous pastor, next to the box of journals found in Sue's vehicle on the night of her death. The box had been taped shut when he received it and it remained that way today. He wasn't sure if he was ready to read his wife's inner thoughts.

Nathan reached for the old books and set the bulk of five on his desk. The top one was an old black leather journal with creases covering the spine and front cover. As he opened the first page, he wrinkled his nose as a musty smell wafted from the open pages.

"*Dated July 20, 1901: My first day as the spiritual head for the townsfolk of Redemption. This is a God-ordained position that will not accept failure. I eagerly anticipate a transition from Reverend Somer to myself, trusting that the Reverend has prepared his flock to receive a new spiritual head. I have been adequately warned regarding the history of this town and understand the grave duty I carry. This town will not turn from the glory of the Lord while under my watchful eye. I know the signs, understand the temperament of an unhealthy church, and will not allow this to happen again."*

The last word leaped out at Nathan. Again. As if the pastor had been through this before. He flipped ahead to the middle of the book, and what he read shocked him.

"November 9, 1902: I have failed. I have lived a lie for the past thirty years. I know the Word of God, yet have not held it as close to my heart as I should. Why else would this tragedy befall me? My faith is weak, my character downtrodden by the temperamental congregation that I serve. My only option is to hand in my resignation. Reverend Somer told me that it was God who appointed the minister to this church built for refuge, but I cannot believe that this post was ordained for me."

Nathan searched the previous pages to see what tragedy happened to this unnamed pastor, and when he found no clue, he searched ahead and only found blank pages. That was the last entry in the journal.

He picked up another journal. This one was dated February 1939, and the minister was Reverend Scheldt. The beginning of the journal sounded similar to the previous one: excited with the new position, full of dreams and aspirations for the church and its community.

Nathan flipped to the middle of the journal and still found a minister who was excited about his calling. It appeared he held a real love for the congregation. He flipped through a few more pages, this time landing almost at the back of the journal. Dated Christmas Day 1941, almost two years into his pastorate, he wrote,

"Christmas Day, a day filled with joy and hope, celebration for the birth of our Savior. Yet today, it is one filled with sadness and despair. Today, instead of celebrating our Savior's birth, I am mourning the loss of my wife. I can find no words to describe my sorrow. My congregation, the same ones who killed my wife, have tried to shelter me,

console me, and hold me up in prayer, but I find their prayers abhor-
rent, their consolation repugnant, and my only wish is to be left in
peace."

Nathan couldn't believe what he was reading. Here was
someone else who understood what he was going through,
someone with whom he could relate. He grabbed the books and
sat down on the couch.

"My beautiful beloved is dead by their blood-drenched hands and
asinine prayers, yet they assume I will continue on with my duties for
the Christmas celebration. I am not that strong, nor that dedicated, it
would seem. I cannot celebrate in the birth of one who would take from
me my very life source. The church will have to learn to celebrate the
life of a God I can only wish dead."

Nathan leaned back and closed his eyes as the grief written
in these old pages overwhelmed him. He wasn't alone.
Someone else who had walked in his shoes years ago understood. He was surprised the journals survived the flood, but he
was glad they did.

After devouring the remaining journals, one theme
remained consistent: a deep loss affected their faith in such a
devastating manner they stepped down from their positions.

The journals mirrored his own journey.

Nathan placed the journal down on the couch, unable to
handle it anymore. He walked over to the bay window and
stared out at his darkened yard. He'd lost hours in those
journals.

As the sun set and cast an aurora as it gently sank behind
the mountain, an overwhelming sense of loneliness set in.

He missed Sue. Things were tense between them at the end,
but he had to believe their love had been real. They would have
been able to work through their issues and rebuild the trust
he'd foolishly destroyed by his omissions.

His gaze followed the colors as they trailed down the side of
the rocky hill and rested on the valley below its feet.

Nathan gasped.

A large black hole hovered in the air. A swirling mass of crows swooped into the hole and then emerged moments later, one after another, as if the currents of the dark opening forced them into a pattern.

He gripped the curtains as the black hole swirled, making its way from the foot of the mountain to the field before him. The grass beneath this mass flattened as it hovered.

Craziness ran in his family. He thought it'd skipped him, but he'd been wrong before.

The cloud stopped at the edge of the field, where it met Nathan's property line. He placed his hand upon the cool glass and recalled the heaviness he'd felt the previous night when he approached the stranger in Kate's diner. He felt that way now.

Nathan raised his hand to wave at the neighbor from across the street who stood on his front lawn, but the look of horror on Nels' face as he held a shovel in his hands had him leaving the glass on the counter and rushing out the door.

As the screen door banged behind him, he immediately noticed the damp chill to the night air.

"Do you see that?" Nels yelled out as he pointed to a few houses down the road.

Nathan stood at the edge of his driveway and peered down the dark street. "What am I looking at? It's almost too dark to see anything that far down."

"You don't see that? My wife thinks it's a UFO. I've been watching it for the past half-hour now." Nels' knuckles tightened around the shovel handle.

Nathan looked down the road again.

About six driveways past his own, there was a dark, hazy image. It was like a swarm of mosquitoes gathering in the dusk for feeding. It moved with slow precision onto the next driveway. A remnant of the swarm stayed in place, reminding him of a sentinel on duty.

"Did you see it move? What is it?" The panic in Nels' voice was more than noticeable.

The swarm continued its way down the street until it stopped one house away from his. A low hum filled the air, and the tiny hairs on Nathan's arms stood up.

At each driveway, a sentinel in the outline of a dark haze hovered above the pavement.

"I have no idea," Nathan admitted.

"Why isn't it coming towards us?" Nels took a step backward and held the shovel away from him.

"Why don't you go back into your house? I'm sure Heather would feel more comfortable with you by her side." Nels' wife was peeking out the front curtain.

Nels held the shovel in both his hands across his chest, nodded, and turned away. He kept glancing behind him before he reached his front door.

Nathan took a step towards the swarm. He watched it move away from him. What was it? A swarm of mosquitoes in search of food or could it be something else entirely?

The closer he came towards the swarm, the further it moved away. He quickened his pace, but the distance between them never changed. When he finally stood on the opposite driveway, the vibrations the swarm gave off intensified.

Nathan stopped.

Something, or someone, protected him.

The black hole he'd seen out his window had stopped at the edge of his property. This dark swarm stayed away from him. Why?

An entry he passed over earlier in one of the journals flashed through his mind. Nathan rushed back into the house and grabbed one of the journals that had fallen to the floor from the couch.

"While the evil one takes residence, the just shall prevail. A town surrounded by darkness will only survive if the spiritual covering remains intact."

There was no spiritual covering over this town anymore. Not like there was back then.

With the variety of churches that filled Redemption, it was impossible to place this burden on one pastor.

But even if you could, placing the burden on him was pointless.

Nathan was finished with God.

When he stepped away from the church, he didn't just relinquish his title and authority. He relinquished his belief as well. And somehow, it felt right.

CHAPTER
SEVENTEEN

THE POUNDING at the front door caught his attention.

He peered through the curtains and saw her pace his front porch. He knocked on the glass. She twirled and beckoned for him to come out. Nathan shook his head. It was late. She could come in.

Except she never did.

The scowl on her face told him it was useless to argue with her.

He rounded the corner of his house and could hear her muttering. "Why is it my job to tell him? This was your decision--"

He scuffed his foot on the rocks loud enough to grab her attention. If she was on the phone, he didn't want to interrupt. Except she wasn't. Her hands were empty, and there was no earpiece either.

"Who are you talking to?"

Eva jumped. "You shouldn't sneak up on people."

Nathan climbed the stairs and then leaned against the railing before crossing his arms. "I didn't."

Eva continued to pace across the porch, her footsteps pounding on the wood.

"I know I need to replace some boards, but I wasn't planning on doing it tonight," Nathan drawled.

Eva stopped in her tracks directly in front of him.

"You know, it's a lot warmer inside my house. One of these days, you'll have to come in."

When she turned, he noticed the tears that ran down her cheeks.

"Ah, Eva..." Nathan held out his arms and waited for her to accept his embrace. What was going on with her? He dropped his arms at the firm shake of her head. He caught the way her shoulders stiffened.

"Today...Nathan...today--"

"Was hell. I know. I was there. Are you okay?"

She shook her head before reaching up and gathering her hair in her hands. With deft fingers, she quickly braided her hair and let it rest against her shoulder. The silky black strands sparkled in the moonlight.

Nathan swallowed and took a moment to compose himself. God, she was beautiful.

"I heard the tree is already gone. The mayor wants a pergola made out of it."

Eva snorted. "Just what this town needs, another monument to the past." She took a step closer to him, her knees bumping into his.

A shot of electricity went up his legs from the slight touch.

"What happened this morning, Eva? I leave you sitting alone in the park, and then not even fifteen minutes later, crows start falling to their death, and I see you lying on the ground." Nathan gripped the rail post in his hands and stared deep into Eva's eyes. He dared her to lie to him. To tell him nothing happened this morning.

When she turned her head and stared out at the road, he'd had enough.

"Damn it, Eva. I need to know what happened. When the tree was about to fall on us, tell me you didn't see that crow rise from the dead! Tell me you didn't hear him. Tell me, damn it, that I'm not going crazy!" It took everything inside of him not to let go of his death grip on the rails and reach out to her.

The sudden feeling of drowning overwhelmed him. She was his anchor, and he needed her. God, he needed her.

She must have heard it in his voice. Her gaze returned to his, her eyes as black as night.

"You're not crazy," she whispered. "Today was a sign. A message meant for you. I just hope you listened." She leaned in and pressed her lips against his before stepping back. A look of sorrow and sadness passed over her features before she turned and ran away from him.

There wasn't time for him to act or even react. Eva had kissed him. Brief as it was, it shook him to the core. He hadn't kissed anyone like that since...Sue.

Nathan whipped his body around at the roar of Eva's motorcycle. Damn her, she couldn't leave. Not now. She didn't answer any of his questions. What did she mean, today was a message for him. Message for what? And from whom? God? He shook his head.

He doubted this was the type of message God would send. Not now. It was too late for him, his soul too black.

CHAPTER
EIGHTEEN

JOANNE

Joanne woke to a blinding light. She tried to close her eyes from the light, hoping for a reprieve from its intense glare.

A parade of shivers traveled over her skin. A black circle crept along her iris, blocking out the light. It reminded her of an eclipse she once peeked at as a child.

Tears formed, creating a sand-like texture within her eyes. She wished she could rub them, blink them, anything to alleviate the dryness in them.

Whispers surrounded her. She tried to distinguish the garbled words, but failed. The sensation of floating underwater while listening to the voices overwhelmed her. She blinked. Surprised, she blinked again. She turned her head and realized nothing held her back - no pain, no restraints.

A soft beep sounded to her left, above where she lay. The smell of the room had changed, yet it was familiar somehow. She knew where she was. The air, with an antiseptic, metallic taste to it, confirmed it.

She wasn't with Max anymore. She was back in her room at

the Mount Joseph Private Hospital. A wave of relief flowed over her.

She turned her head towards the door and stared at the back of a white doctor's coat. The soft glow around the man reassured her. Everything was fine. She could see. Thank you, Jesus. She could see.

Tears streamed down her face as she took in the drawings she made and taped them to her wall, the pictures of Nathan as a child she'd kept, and the row of journals on her single white bookshelf.

A low murmur caught her attention. She strained to hear what was being said but could only make out a few words.

"Not strong enough."

Joanne stiffened. She recognized the voice.

Then remembered.

"Yes, Doctor. I understand." The soft voice of Joanne's favorite nurse reached her ears. Shelly. She could help her. Shelly was always there with her, listening to her. She would understand. She had to.

She raised her arm up to catch Shelley's attention, but the doctor took two steps back, glanced over his shoulder, and smiled.

She knew those eyes. She'd recognize them anywhere.

She wasn't safe. Not here. Not anymore. She knew exactly where she was.

In hell. With the devil named Morax.

CHAPTER
NINETEEN

NATHAN

The heavens opened and a deluge of rain poured. Dusty paths turned to mud as families ran, young children gathered in their arms as they dashed across the park to the shelter of their vehicles. Nathan decided to wait for the rain to slack off and stepped back until he stood under the Town Hall overhang. Jack and Kate joined him.

"You need to find Rachel," Kate said.

"I've tried, Kate." Nathan shook his head and stared out at the empty grounds. The heavy pour turned into a light spattering of rain, until mist swirls gathered above the blades of grass blanketing the park. An eerie feeling permeated the air.

"I haven't heard from her all day. She won't return my phone calls." Nathan stuck his hands in his pockets and shrugged back his shoulders. He was so tight. It had been a few days since he last went for a good run, and he was feeling it.

It bothered him more than he wanted to admit that Rachel had gone quiet on him.

She'd been shaken after the tree had fallen yesterday. He

should have checked up on her afterward instead of leaving her alone as he had.

When Kate didn't answer, he turned. Her arms crossed her ample chest, and the fiercest frown filled her face. Her eyes shifted away as he stared.

"You might as well tell him, woman." Jack laid his arm across Kate's shoulders and squeezed.

Nathan rubbed his chin. "Tell me what? Do you know where she is but haven't said anything?"

"She went to the cabin." Kate's head lowered at the words.

He jerked in surprise. Cabin? There was only one cabin Rachel had ever mentioned, and he knew she would never go there. Not willingly, at least. "You let her go?"

Kate lifted her head, tears brimming over her lashes. She didn't answer.

Damn it.

"Why didn't she tell me? Why would she go up there alone?"

Jack growled. Nathan glared at him.

"Said you had your own demons to worry about, you didn't need to deal with hers as well." Kate's lips tightened into a straight line.

Nathan didn't know how to respond to that. He deserved it.

"Why?" Why would she go up to the one place she abhorred?

Kate shook her head. "Her Pa used to read stories to her at night from an old journal he had. Ghost stories from the previous owner. Stories from the past. She remembered one about the myth in there. She thought it might have some answers."

Nathan shook his head. Why didn't she call him? She'd be out of cell phone range, so it made sense why she never answered when he called. It didn't explain why she would go alone.

"When did she leave?"

Kate bit her lip. When Jack nudged her, he knew he wouldn't like what she had to say.

"Yesterday. After the tree fell and you'd left."

Instant anger burned through his body. He wanted to hit something, someone. He'd never felt this way before. Ever.

His relationship with Rachel was nothing like he'd ever experienced before, especially not with Sue.

They didn't call each other all the time or spend every waking moment together. Nathan wanted to take his time building their relationship.

When he met Sue, he'd fallen in love right away. He proposed after six months, and they were married 4 months later in a small country church. He swore before God that he'd love his wife forever, and look where it left him. He didn't deserve someone like Rachel in his life. But it was her kindness, her innocence, and honesty that wrapped itself around his heart until the walls he'd built were starting to crumble. He fought that crumbling every day. And look where it left him.

To know she hadn't trusted him enough with this burned like fire at his heart. And he was the only one to blame.

He was a fool.

"Seems to me you need to decide what she means to you. You've got to make a choice, boy. You can't have two women in your life, in your heart. It's not fair to either one of them." Jack shook his head before he entwined his fingers with Kate's. The mist had made its way up to the third step, but the older couple ignored it.

"What if I don't make the right choice?" Nathan called out.

"You will. Now go find her," Jack called over his shoulder. Nathan watched the gentle way Jack handled his wife, and as they disappeared into the fog, he realized just how alone he was.

He pulled out his phone and tried Rachel's number again. This time the only message heard was the automated voice telling him her mailbox was full.

Nathan stuck the phone back in his pants pocket and stared out at the empty park in front of him. "Dammit, Rachel. Why couldn't you have trusted me enough?"

The rain slowed till it became a drizzle. As Nathan headed down the stairs, an opening in the mist appeared. Tendrils of the fog swirled out and wrapped around his ankles.

He knew it wasn't possible, but he would swear something was pulling at his feet. He picked up the pace and continued down the walk. The fog billowed around him, leaving the stone pathway clear. He could only see about eight feet ahead of him, but he knew he should be close to Main Street.

Thunder rumbled, and flashes of lightning filled the darkened sky and illuminated the shadowy figure of a man standing directly in front of him. Nathan stumbled before he caught himself.

The man in black from the diner.

The demon.

Something about him pulled at Nathan.

There was only one thing to do. Keep walking.

He wasn't sure if it was the mist from the fog swirling at his feet or what, but the smell of sulfur intensified the closer he came to the apparition.

Nathan refused to look at him, so he focused on the street ahead. He held his breath as he drew near and struggled not to gag as he passed the silent figure.

"I have her. Rachel is mine."

The man's raspy voice sent shivers along Nathan's body. He whipped his head around, but he'd disappeared. A lone crow stood in his place, its beady eyes blinking.

Join me.

Nathan almost fell to his knees as the words whispered around him, the cadence rising and falling as the words repeated over and over in his mind.

He stumbled to the nearest bench and grabbed hold until his knuckles turned white.

He was going crazy. He knew it. Just like his mother. First, the crows; next, it would be rats or snakes. No way. Not him. Oh God, please don't let him be like his mother.

Nathan whipped his head around to face the crow who dared to mess with his mind.

The street was empty.

CHAPTER
TWENTY

WITHIN MINUTES of him exiting Redemption, a surge of rain poured from the heavens, and the swoosh of the windshield wipers did little to clear his view.

Nathan's knuckles were white as he gripped the steering wheel, barely able to see anything on the road. The clouded black sky hid the moon from view, and if he didn't know better, he would have sworn it was midnight.

Tension flowed through his blood as he inched along the highway. The further he drove into the mountains, the tighter the curves got. The sharp drop-off into jagged ravines and streams were death traps on nights like this.

He stifled the urge to drive faster.

As he rounded a corner, the lights from his truck highlighted a large black mass in the middle of the road. Nathan stomped on his brakes, and sections of the mass flew into the air.

Damn crows. Again.

The sound of their high-pitched cawing overpowered the drum of rain on the roof of his truck. The symphony from hell pounded until the air thickened with their cries. Fear slithered along Nathan's skin, covering him with its slimy presence. He shuddered.

He didn't want to drive through the murder of crows. The memory of the last time this scene played out still haunted him. The need to find Rachel conquered the drive of fear, and he laid on the horn and sneered as more crows lifted off the road, their frantic black wings beating the air.

A flash of red caught his eye as he watched some crows join a large group circling in the sky. He jammed his truck in park and leaned over to catch a better glimpse. He struggled to see into the shadowed ravine, but a few of the birds swooped down and aimed straight for his passenger window. He could have sworn the beady eyes of the demonic birds glowed red.

He reached across, opened his glove compartment, and grabbed a flashlight. He flicked it on and aimed the light out the window. When the crows shied away from the light, Nathan aimed the light towards the red object he saw in the bush.

Rachel drove a red pickup.

Nathan pushed the driver's door open and scrambled out of the truck. He might not have been able to save his wife, but he would save Rachel.

He had to.

A large black shape swooped down towards the hood of the truck. Nathan ducked. As the bird flew past, Nathan detected a sulfuric stench. He lifted his arm and held his sleeve over his nose while digging into his pants pocket for his cell phone.

He called the sheriff's office, and while he waited for someone to answer, he rushed back to his truck for his emergency first aid kit and whispered the first prayer he'd uttered in the past few years.

"God, please let Rachel be alive."

A burst of wind hit him full in the face as he edged up to the front of the truck. With his phone propped to his ear, he lifted his forearm to shield his eyes from any potential attacks from the swooping crows.

"Redemption Sheriff's Department," Mavis, the night switchboard operator, answered.

"I'm out on Lost Lake Road. I think Rachel's in the ravine. Send the ambulance and tow truck. Just be careful, there are strange things going on out here," Nathan said as he rushed to the edge of the road.

"Nathan, is that you? You found Rachel?" The tell-tale slap of chewing gum smacked in his ear.

"I'm sure it's her truck."

"I'll radio the Sheriff now. Hang tight, sugar."

Nathan took a deep breath to calm himself as he peered into the dark abyss. Too many people died on these treacherous mountain roads. People like Sue.

"Rachel? Can you hear me?" Nathan yelled as loud as he could.

With his first step, he slid five feet downwards. Nathan struggled to grab tree branches or even hook his shoes on exposed roots as he slid further down the sharp decline, but the rain-slicked his hands so much that everything slipped through his grip. Blasts of haunting cries filled the area as the seedy crows circled above the tree line. Nathan had never been more thankful for a shrouded area than now.

The sight of the truck wrapped around a tree had Nathan dry-heaving. The smell of gas was overpowering.

He grabbed onto the edge of the crumpled metal for support and made his way to the driver's door.

"Rachel, can you hear me?" He pulled on the handle and wrenched the door open. She lay slumped over the steering wheel.

The sight of her lying there, lifeless, scared him. She couldn't be dead. He wouldn't let her be.

"Oh, God. Rachel, please be okay. I can't lose you," Nathan whispered as he leaned inside to brush aside her hair to check her pulse. That's when he noticed the dark patches of blood coating her hair.

His hands shook as he placed his two fingers on her neck. Nothing. No pulse. No life.

"No." Nathan choked back a sob.

He couldn't lose her. An uncontrollable rage swept over him. How dare God do this to him?

What kind of sick, twisted games was God playing?

Nathan had had enough.

"Damn you. Who the hell do you think you are taking another woman I love away from me?" he cried.

As he held back his tears, Nathan gently gathered Rachel in his arms and pulled her away from the steering wheel. The blue pallor of her lips chilled his heart.

The distant sounds of sirens filled the air. Nathan glanced over his shoulder for the lights, but the darkness held its secrets.

He bent forward and placed a gentle kiss on her cheek. He let the tears flow unchecked. He couldn't believe the crushing love that swept over him for this woman. And she was dead.

He was too late.

He gazed up into the night sky and stared straight into the black, soulless eyes of a crow.

Join us, Nephilim, son of Morax.

He couldn't take it anymore.

Nathan screamed a deep guttural sound that tore his throat apart. He released his hold on Rachel and gripped the driver's door and with one pull, he ripped it off the truck and threw it at the crows circling above him.

The bird swerved out of the way and settled on the truck roof. It hopped out of Nathan's reach.

Stronger than anticipated. Not what you seem. More than anticipated. Join us, before he comes for you.

"What are you?" Nathan yelled as he slammed his clenched fist on the roof. A large indent bowed beneath his hand. He couldn't handle this anymore. His knees buckled beneath him. He turned his gaze from the crow to Rachel and hit the ground with a thud.

Rachel. Dead.

He covered his face with his hands as a deep retching sob shook his body.

He should have saved her. Why didn't she trust him enough to tell him where she was going?

Because he didn't deserve her trust.

Why should she tell him where she was going? Not even Sue had done that.

The night Sue died, he'd been at the church working on a sermon. They'd argued earlier in the day about a bill that had arrived. A bill Sue had no idea Nathan paid on a monthly basis.

To Mount Joseph Private Hospital.

Instead of telling Sue the truth about his mother after she accused him of not trusting her, he'd stormed out and refused to answer any of her calls or text messages. He stayed as long as he could at the church, hoping that Sue would have gone to bed before he got home.

He hadn't wanted to face the truth. Instead, his fears were exposed.

The faint glow of lights drew his attention. Criss-cross beams shone down the ravine, illuminating the slippery slope.

Help was here. But it was too late.

"Down here." Nathan scrambled to his feet and waved his arms until the flashlights blinded him with their brightness.

He cast one last look at Rachel and memorized the deathly mask that replaced the life, the sparkle, and the joy of a woman who deserved more than this.

His heart broke as he whispered her name.

Nathan recognized the paramedics as they made their way down the bank. He stepped back and out of the way as they bypassed him and focused on Rachel.

He noticed the concerned glances sent his way, but it didn't matter. His stoic attitude was all he could handle. He knew he detached himself from reality. It was the only way he could survive right now.

As he helped carry her up the slippery embankment, he

caught the winged flight of the crows out of the corner of his eye. He refused to listen to their whispered beckoning.

The thud of the ambulance door as it closed behind Rachel's body was the final straw. His feet cemented into the ground as he lifted his face to the cloud-filled sky. His scream echoed off of the rock face and taunted him.

When he faced his truck, fiery anger filled him. He bent down and scooped up small rocks around his feet. One at a time, he threw stones at the murder of crows that covered his truck.

"Get. Away. From. Me," he ground out between clenched teeth. His chest heaved as the rocks bounced off of his truck without hitting a single bird.

Journals hold the key.

Nathan darted towards the truck and flailed his arms. The crows swept up in a swirl of cascading feathers and circled high above him.

He yanked open his door and threw himself inside the cab. His nostrils flared as he struggled to calm his breathing. He needed to get a hold of himself and head home before he lost it for good.

Nephilim. Son of Morax. Listen--

Nathan jerked the key in the ignition and rammed his foot on the gas pedal.

CHAPTER
TWENTY-ONE

THE GLARE of headlights blinded him as he sped home. He barely caught the outline of a woman's silhouette before he jammed on the brakes.

Throwing his vehicle into park, Nathan jumped out and slammed the door.

"Damn it, woman, don't you know I could have hit you!"

"You wouldn't have." Eva wiped the rain off her face and stared at him. "I'm so sorry, Nathan—"

"No!" He shouted. He turned on his heels, wishing he could turn his back on everything and everyone. He couldn't go through this again. Not again.

"It's not your fault." Eva's hand gripped his arm and stopped him.

He shrugged it off. "Like hell, it isn't. She should never have come out here on her own. She didn't trust me enough to go with her. I could have saved her!" The flood burst, and tears streamed down his face.

Eva shook her head. "No, you couldn't have." She reached out to him and rested the palm of her hand against his face. Her thumb gently stroked his skin.

"There's nothing you could have done, Nathan. She wasn't

for you. She was never meant for you." Her voice, a silken whisper, surrounded his soul, soothing away the anger that consumed him.

"What do you mean?" Nathan stared deep into Eva's eyes and found himself lost. Visions of his life with her, with Eva, flashed before him.

"You are more than what you think you are. So much more. Those crows speak to you because they need you. They can help, Nathan. They can help you understand what is happening to you. What will happen to you..."

"What will...what are you talking about?"

Her lips curled into a half smile before she raised her other hand and rested a finger against his lips.

"Find that journal. Then you'll understand. I promise." She stepped backward, her gaze never leaving hers, until she stood beside her motorcycle. "I'm always here, Nathan. Always. I'll never give up on you."

He waited until she sped away on her motorcycle before turning away and sitting back in his truck. He pounded the steering wheel in frustration.

I'll never give up on you. What did she mean by that?

There was nothing he could do for Rachel. She was gone. So was his chance at redemption. There was no turning back now. Nothing left for him to return to.

He knew exactly what journal the damn crow and Eva meant.

It was time to delve into the past and find some answers. No matter what hell it led him to.

CHAPTER
TWENTY-TWO

MORAX

Morax sat in the corner chair of the study and watched his son pull the battered box off the top shelf. He rubbed his hands and resisted the urge to snicker. He'd waited a long time for his son to open that particular box.

All his plans had been made for this one moment.

The grief etched on Nathan's face did little to soften his heart. Grief was a human emotion meant as a crutch for the weak. His son was anything but.

He made sure he'd seen to that. What was one death compared to the survival of a species?

Morax leaned back and lifted his arms behind his head. With his legs crossed, he settled back to watch the beginning of Nathan's transformation.

There weren't many Nephilim alive. The odds of one living to their fortieth year were miraculous. The enemy did everything possible to ensure they didn't survive to the year of maturing.

But Nathan was different. There was a special quality about

his DNA that no other Nephilim had because of Morax's genius. He wasn't called the president of Hell or the demonic god of science for nothing. Genetic mutations were his creations.

Like his son. Like Eva. Created for each other to rule where no fallen angel had dared. Like this silly little town he created.

Morax leaned forward as Nathan pulled out the journal his mother had written all those years ago. A journal full of research on the Nephilim, on fallen angels, on the women who succumbed to the seduction of angels.

Everything was for this one moment.

In order for the rest of his plans to be put into action, Morax had needed Nathan destroyed.

The death of his wife and now the weak woman he was foolishly falling in love with guaranteed the demise of any pastoral longings his son might still retain.

He'd been mistaken to rely on Eva to lead Nathan in the right direction. Despite being a creature of his own making, he should have known not to trust her. Not when her heart was involved. She had two years to prepare Nathan for what was to come. Two years wasted when his son could have been training and learning.

Preparing to rule.

Morax shook his head. He'd been the laughingstock of the council when they'd learned his son was a minister of the Most High God. Anger welled inside him at the memory.

They wouldn't be laughing now, not when his son became the savior of their species.

It all depended on the journal and the ripped page Morax held in his hands. The page containing all the answers to the questions his son would soon have.

A sickening smile grew as he watched the horror of knowledge spread across Nathan's face.

This was just the beginning...

PART TWO
THE PROTECTOR

EVA SINE

CHAPTER
TWENTY-THREE

EVA

Nathan was missing.

Eva paced across her living room floor, her hands clenching at her sides. Irritation swelled up inside of her.

Waiting was never her strongest feature.

She grabbed the one framed photo she had of Nathan and wanted to fling it across the room. How dare he leave her like this. Didn't he realize what he was doing to her? How much he meant to her? Who did he think he was to take off and not say anything?

She was his mate, his lifeline. At least, she should be.

What if he didn't come back in time? She bit her lip at the thought and tasted blood on her tongue. For the first time in a long time, Eva was groundless.

Everything she'd known no longer mattered with Nathan off the grid. She couldn't sense him, feel him, or even hear him.

It scared her, and she didn't do well with being scared.

Ever since that night on the road, after Nathan found Rachel at the bottom of the ravine, he'd been a changed man.

Cold. Hard. Sheltered.

She almost couldn't read him, he'd been so closed off to her.

She'd tried to steer him in the right direction, but she had no idea if he even heard her. At Rachel's funeral, he'd refused to talk to her as she stood beside him at the cemetery, and he took off before anyone could approach him.

She'd waited on his front porch for hours, but he never came home.

Eva stopped dead in her tracks as she felt another presence in the room. A heaviness filled the air that hadn't been there before. Eva headed to her front door and gripped the knob.

She steeled herself, straightened her spine, and smoothed her hair down.

The fact it stood outside didn't surprise her. She knew who it was. After all, she'd been the one to summon it.

The moment she opened her door, a brisk breeze enveloped her, flicking her red scarf across her chest. She reached for her leather jacket and shimmied into it before stepping outside.

Where is he? The deathly voice from the pale being that stood at the edge of her small concrete porch wove around her. The tendrils of poison released from its open mouth were visible, wisps of black and grey with a tint of red streaks.

With her hand tight on the door handle, she challenged it as the deadly stain wound into an intricate pattern around the cacodaemon before hitting her shield.

She wasn't stupid. Playing nice with the enemy didn't mean playing stupid.

Eva shrugged her shoulder at the soulless creature.

"You weren't supposed to kill her." Eva maintained a sense of indifference. A necessity in the face of hell. One sign of weakness, and the cacodaemon would use it against her.

We didn't.

Eva stepped back in surprise. Who then?

Who would kill Rachel, knowing she was the only thing

keeping Nathan from turning into the Nephilim he was created to be before he should?

"I don't believe you."

The cacodaemon growled in warning, its normal blank features edged in anger. For a moment, Eva would have sworn she'd seen the outline of a face behind the blank mask.

The first time she'd seen the unnatural being, she'd stared for the longest time, trying to see the face she knew should be there. But now she just flipped him the finger before heading to her bike.

Where is he?

Eva turned and faced the demon behind her. A shiver ran down her spine. She hated these things.

"At the bottom of some cliff, for all I know. You," she poked her finger at the demon's chest only to have her finger go straight through. Gross. "You were supposed to stick close to him. Keep an eye on him. Remember?"

That is your job, Restorer of Nephilim.

Anger boiled within her veins. How she hated that word.

She was an abomination, a castoff to their species.

She was female. Created for only one purpose. For only one being. Nathan. Who, at that very moment, was in the midst of turning from a human into a supernatural being.

"First off, you've got your facts wrong, buddy. I'm not the Restorer. I'm his mate. Second, my job is to help him turn, which I can't do because of you. You killed the one tether he had left to this town, the town where he is supposed to be protected. Or did you forget that tiny little detail?" She stared down the nameless creature, refusing to be pulled into its depths. She may not be a human, angel, or even a demon, but she had her own level of powers gifted to her.

Thanks to her father. Her creator.

We did not kill the Nephilim's love. The town still holds its purpose. The Restorer is still protected.

Eva's brow rose. What's up with this restorer nonsense?

She knew Morax had high hopes for Nathan, it was all he ever talked about. But for the cacodaemon to label him as such before he'd turned, that said a lot.

Too much, actually.

"He's not The Restorer. Not yet." Her eyes narrowed. At the slight raise of the creature's thin lips, Eva knew she'd just lost that battle. She'd shown a weakness.

Many things are kept hidden until the day of revealing. Restorer.

She swore she heard the mirth in its voice. Damn the thing.

If Morax hadn't ordered her to work with the vile creature, she would have sent it back to hell where it belonged.

Instead, she turned on her heel and made for her bike. Nathan did love her, just not completely. Not the way she needed him to. But he would. And, when he did, she would be there for him, accepting him for who he was and what he was about to become.

"You may not realize it yet, Nathan Hanlin - but your destiny goes beyond the little pulpit in your old church. The choice is still yours to make, if you even make it in time." She murmured as she kick-started her bike. A quick glance to her left confirmed the demon had disappeared.

She needed to find Nathan before it did.

She knew he wasn't at his house. She'd placed enough safe-guards around the place that she would have picked up his presence if he were.

And, if he were within Redemption town limits she would sense him, she always had.

Since she couldn't hear even the barest of whispers or sense him at all, he must be beyond her reach. She twisted her long hair into a quick braid and tucked one end of her red scarf into her leather jacket before reaching for her helmet.

She was going to find him. No matter what it took.

CHAPTER
TWENTY-FOUR

NATHAN

It took the insistent chatter of a damn crow in his head for Nathan Hanlin to finally come to grips with the idea he was going crazy.

It was the only answer, nothing else made sense.

As much as he didn't want to admit it, he was more like his mother than he thought.

His mother could see demons, he could hear them.

Like mother like son.

A faint light flashed between the slivers of wood boards covering the front windows of the house. His shoulders slumped as he stared out the driver's side window. Nothing made sense to him. Not the talking crows or the flashes of blue and white coming from a house that had been deserted for more years than he wanted to admit.

What was he doing here?

The rash decision made at Rachel's funeral now seemed pointless. This dilapidated shack couldn't possibly hold the answers he was looking for, even if he knew the questions to ask.

Gone were the days when he knew who he was and what he was. Nathan snorted. What, being the optimum word. He used to be a pastor. Now he was what, an angel? A demon? Or was he something in between?

Was that even possible?

Nathan's fingers gripped the steering wheel until his white knuckles ached. He'd lost count of time since he'd first parked his Jeep across from the deserted building. He exhaled into the cold vehicle and stared, mesmerized at the white fog that circled in front of him before dissipating into nothing.

This house drew him. Called to him. Visions of this place filled his dreams. After the nightmare of the crows circling over Rachel's truck had come true, there was no way he was ignoring this one.

Maybe, just maybe, if he'd paid attention before, Rachel would be alive.

Guilt ate at him. It was all his fault.

If only he'd known, both Rachel and Sue would be alive.

A beaten box sat beside him on the other seat. The lid, propped open for easy access, had slid down into the little space between the seat and the passenger door. Nathan didn't care. All that mattered were the puzzle pieces it contained.

Three crows stood guard on the front porch of the house he watched. They stared at him, their unblinking eyes unnerving him, taunting him to take the first step.

Nathan picked up a journal lying in his lap. It was all in here. Every deep, dark secret his mother had kept from him. Stories from the bible that he barely believed—all in graphic detail.

His mother had known it all along. She knew, but she never told him. He'd lived a lie his whole life, and the only one to blame was himself.

Not his mother, who kept the secrets from him. Not his wife, who was going to leave him. Not God or Satan, whichever one had created him.

No. Nathan could only lay the blame at his own feet.

The answers had been in front of him the whole time, but he'd ignored them.

Images of Rachel's funeral played over in his mind. The somber atmosphere over those who mourned the death of an innocent. An innocent whose only desire was to save the lives of others. Nathan hadn't deserved her love, something he'd realized as her body was lowered into the ground and handfuls of dirt dropped over her casket.

He'd stood there, watching guard until dusk had fallen, and he was alone. A part of him died that night, buried deep in the ground. As he'd walked back to his vehicle, he realized something.

The man he knew--the pastor who wanted to believe that God, in all his infinite wisdom, had a plan--no longer existed.

Nephilim. Arise.

Nathan breathed the frigid air into his lungs, as he threw the journal in his hand, back into the opened box. The man he knew gave way to the man he was today.

Cold. Empty. Determined. He was tired of playing games when he didn't know the rules. Enough was enough.

If the crows wanted to dance, he'd be the one to pick the tune. He'd be the one controlling the strings, playing the puppet master.

They wanted the Nephilim. What they would get was him. Nathan Hanlin.

The light flashed again.

Nathan flung open the driver's door and unfolded his body from the vehicle. Blood circulated, and tiny pinpricks of needles covered his skin. He relished the pain, craved it.

Come to us Nephilim, son of Morax. Join us.

Nathan crossed the street, his steps determined.

He had sworn never to return here -- too many secrets, too

much heartbreak. He made a promise he could no longer keep. Some promises are meant to be broken. Some secrets needed to be exposed.

Whatever was inside, whoever was inside was about to get a rude awakening.

Nathan had come home.

CHAPTER
TWENTY-FIVE

EVA

She loved the feel of the wind as it swirled around her. Being on her bike was as close to flying as she could get. The rush from the high speeds as she gained momentum, facing death with every curve, was exhilarating, except for today.

She took her time driving down the highway, mentally searching for even a glimmer of confirmation that Nathan was nearby. Nothing. No tendril of a wayward thought. No nudge. Just silence.

She couldn't stand it. Uneasiness ate at her from the inside out. Her stomach was in knots, and just thinking about the emptiness inside her made her want to be sick.

From the very beginning, there had always been a presence, a feeling of not being alone. A connection. It used to annoy the hell of her. Being programmed from the very beginning for one person went against everything.

Eva was brought up to be in control, a person with control, a person of authority.

Until she met Nathan.

The first time she was only six. They'd built a sandcastle together on the crowded beach of Redemption Lake.

The next time she'd just turned thirteen. Dusk had fallen, and she'd been walking along the boardwalk, listening to the seagulls and enjoying the rare moment of freedom. Nathan had been throwing a football across the beach with a friend. He didn't even notice her presence.

The last time she'd seen Nathan before moving to Redemption was on his wedding day.

She needed to witness the vows he'd speak to another woman for herself - a woman not created for him, yet one he somehow loved. She'd slipped into the church just moments before Sue entered on the arm of her father. It took only one look for her to realize why Nathan had fallen in love with a human. Her pure heart drew him in. She knew he struggled with inner demons he didn't understand and thought to will them away by becoming a minister.

Eva had walked out of the church determined to help Nathan live the life he chose, not the one forced upon him. Even if it meant she wasn't able to live the life she wanted.

She loved him that much. She always would.

The small county limits sign was up ahead and Eva slowed her bike until whipping it in a half circle just in front of the sign. Rocks flew, leaving dents in the faded green metal. Driving beyond the county border was useless. There were limits in place even she couldn't cross. Until they were mated, this was one of them.

Glancing down the road, Eva searched as far as she could within her mind, but the emptiness remained. She didn't want to consider what it meant. She couldn't. So instead, she sped back down the road she'd just traveled, trying to think of what to do next.

Only one thought plagued her. Eva bit her lip. No. She

wasn't doing that. Wasn't going there. There had to be another option.

But she'd be damned if she could think of what it was.

CHAPTER
TWENTY-SIX

THE LOCAL SHERIFF waited for her as she whizzed by the 'Welcome to Redemption' sign.

Catching the flash of lights in her mirror, Eva smirked as she led him into town before pulling into the parking lot of the small town cafe. She hooked her bike helmet to the small box at the backend of her bike, fluffed her hair, and waited for the stern talking she knew was about to come.

"Ms. Sine, you know you can't be driving at those speeds, not within Redemption," the soft southern drawl she'd been waiting for had goosebumps run up and down her arms.

No one knew the handsome, southern devil quite like Eva did.

Most considered the Sheriff to be an upright kind of guy. Appearances can be deceiving, however.

Beneath the gentle facade was a fallen angel who could and had killed with a simple thought. Even Eva had been known to be scared of him at a time or two.

Eva leaned back against her bike and crossed her arms, giving off a devil-may-care attitude despite the glare in his eyes. "Now Cam, you know I wasn't actually in Redemption." She batted her eyelashes at him and stifled her laughter as his brows knit together. When his lips tightened, she knew she was in trouble. "I was past the town limits, Sheriff Bryant, just like you asked."

At the shake of his head, Eva leaned forward and rested her hand on his arm. She wasn't prepared for the emotional assault she experienced from the touch. Anger boiled deep below the surface, and she had a feeling it was directed at her.

"I can't find Nathan, and I wasn't paying attention," she said softly, hoping those words alone would explain her behavior.

Apologizing didn't come easy for her, especially when it came to Cam, who was a stickler for following the rules and staying within the imaginary lines drawn in the sand.

For him, it meant staying out of trouble and keeping those he guarded safe. For her, it meant living a boring life.

"If you can't find him, then no one can." A low growl escaped through Cam's clenched teeth. His boot scuffed against the gravel driveway. The anger within Cam intensified, and Eva released his arm in alarm before taking a step back.

The tension and power he controlled beneath his calm demeanor cracked through. Cam Bryant was no ordinary Sheriff. He was also her guardian.

Eva held her hands up in front of her. "It's been three days. I've driven along every back road and visited every camping ground along the shoreline, but there's been nothing. I know he's not dead," she shook her head as Cam glared at her. "Morax would have been all over our asses if he was."

Cam took a step towards her, anger rolling off his body in waves and slamming into her own. "Find him."

The command demolished whatever tenuous hold Eva managed to have left of her anger. She jabbed her finger into his chest. She didn't care who witnessed their altercation. "And, how exactly am I supposed to do that, oh mighty one? The damn cacodaemon assigned to him can't even locate him."

"How do you know that?" There was a deadly steel laced to his words.

Eva's brow rose. What? Cam didn't expect her to keep tabs on the demons? Like hell, she wasn't.

"I summoned the demon to my place. I wanted him to know that he's not the one in charge here. Yet the damn thing had the gall to suggest this mess we're in is my fault." Eva drew in the air with her finger and created a small circular flame, a child's game among those of her kind.

She stared at the blazing sphere, mesmerized by its rotational design. Just as expected, Bryant slashed at her hand and stepped backward, jerking his head towards the cafe windows located behind them. Eva resisted the urge to look over her shoulder. No doubt they had an audience. It was Redemption, after all.

"You're crossing a line, Eva. Don't push me." His lips curled back.

Eva crossed her arms and raised her eyebrow. "Or what? Your threats are groundless. Morax needs me too much. You," she winked, "need me too much. Or, have you forgotten that?"

The glare in Cam's eyes receded as a smirk covered his face. "You need to try a different tactic, your reputation is proving to be more of a hindrance than anticipated. You need this town to love you. Now, more than ever." He turned and headed back to his squad car. "It's time," he called over his shoulder.

Eva hissed. "He's not ready."

"Then make him." Cam slammed the driver's door and backed out of the cafe parking lot, leaving Eva seething. She reached for her helmet only to be stopped by the jingle of the cafe diner's bell.

"Eva, come inside." Kate held the door open. Eva cocked her head as she struggled to reign in the swell of anger and terror that coursed through her. Everything she'd worked so hard for was unraveling right in front of her, and there was nothing she could do.

"I won't invite you again," Kate said.

Go in. Overhead, the caw of a crow sounded.

What happened to a person having the choice? Why did she feel like all her options were being taken away even before she had the chance to make a decision?

With a sigh, Eva pushed herself away from the bike and headed towards Kate, the one woman in the whole town who never bothered to hide her disdain for her.

CHAPTER
TWENTY-SEVEN

ALL EYES WERE on Eva as she entered the small cafe. Straightening her shoulders, she schooled her features to show her indifference. She'd worked hard to earn the reputation she had.

Until now, no one else in this town had really mattered to her. Her sole focus was Nathan. She could use an angel in disguise if there was one around, God knows she needed the help right now.

If do-overs were possible, maybe, just maybe, she'd have done things a little bit differently. But she'd known the moment she met Rachel she could never compete. Not with her bubbly attitude and pure heart. Why bother trying when the town angel already wore the crown of gold?

Besides, her 'bad girl' persona suited her purposes. When Nathan turned, he would need a woman who understood what he was going through.

Not many had survived turning from human to Nephilim. The transformation started from the inside out, remolding the organs, tissues, and muscles.

The last Nephilim to survive the transformation had been

killed in battle. According to Morax, if the transformation didn't kill them, the angelic guard would.

The only reason she was still alive is because she was born a Nephilim. Cam used to tease her that she wasn't strong enough to survive the turn, so Morax had pity on her and started her off as one.

Why men continued to think of women as the weaker sex boggled her mind.

As she gazed around the cafe, she realized that maybe Cam was right. There wasn't one single smile of welcome from anyone in the cafe as she followed Kate.

She recognized many of the people, having run into them at one time or another. She'd lived in the town for over two years, yet never felt welcomed or even wanted unless she was with Nathan.

And even then, it was a feigned acceptance.

She made sure to look everyone in the eye and smile. Maybe it was time to try a different tactic. Besides, the crown of gold had to sit on someone's head. Why not hers?

Having Kate on her side might just be the ticket.

"How about a piece of chocolate cake along with that cup of coffee?" Kate slid a white mug in front of an empty stool at the counter and poured coffee into it. Eva glanced around and noticed the front counter to be completely void of any guests.

"Is it homemade?" Eva's mouth watered as Kate lifted the glass dome off the cake stand. The sweet chocolate aroma wafted over. It had been a long time since Eva had enjoyed anything homemade. Her baking skills were sorely lacking.

"As if I would offer anything less."

Eva caught the note of censor in Kate's voice. She offered an apologetic smile before leaning forward and eyeing the slice Kate arranged on a plate for her. She couldn't wait to dig her fork into the decadent dessert. The last time she'd indulged in a piece of chocolate cake was the kind you buy in the freezer section. She's spent her teenage years learning how to destroy a demon with a thought instead of learning how to make the perfect soufflé like the other girls in town.

"This is the first cake I've served that wasn't baked by Rachel."

With her fork raised, Eva lifted her eyes and looked at the woman in front of her. Really looked at her. Sorrow bled through her soul as her back bowed and her shoulders caved inward. The warrior Eva always thought Kate to be, had disappeared.

"She was a daughter to you." Eva set her fork down. She tried to say it with sincerity, but the sarcasm seeped through.

Kate shook her head. "She was more than that, and you know it."

Eva eyed the cake before sighing and pushing it slightly in front of her. No matter how delicious it looked, it would taste like sawdust in her mouth. Rachel's death was her fault. She should have thought to have protected her.

"I'm sorry, Kate. Rachel didn't deserve to die." She'd said the same thing to Nathan at the funeral.

The bell over the cafe door jingled. Eva kept her gaze locked on Kate.

"You're right. She didn't deserve to die. She gave up her life to try to save a man she loved. Would you do the same thing?"

The sudden silence in the cafe was deafening.

Rage boiled inside of Eva, from a place so deep she knew if she didn't do something soon, she'd say or do something she'd regret.

She needed Nathan. He was what kept her grounded, whether he knew it or not.

The sharp caw of a crow from outside the store windows reminded her she wasn't alone, however.

She took a deep breath before reaching for the cake. She counted to five before lifting the fork and slicing it through the dessert. Schooling her features so that Kate wouldn't realize how much her words affected her, she tried to smile before sliding the fork into her mouth.

Sawdust would have tasted better.

"Nathan is my life," Eva whispered. Kate took a step back. "Giving up my life for him isn't an option. Making sure he lives is." She couldn't do this.

"That's always been my goal."

Standing, she turned and stared at every single person in the cafe, making note of the shocked looks on their faces. There were enough people here to help get the word out about her. Not many, but it was a step, at least.

"I'm not...evil. I'm just a woman in love with a man who..." She didn't bother to finish her sentence.

The silence in the little cafe was palatable. An awkward cough from the back of the cafe broke the moment.

"Sit down, child," Kate muttered while shaking her head, her tight curls bouncing at the motion.

Eva sighed and sat back down on the red vinyl stool, and reached for her cup of black coffee.

She hated black coffee. "Milk or creamer?"

Eva cringed at the little creamers in the dish Kate pushed towards her and shook her head. "Flavoured?" It was the only way she could stomach the taste.

Kate snorted.

The crow cawed again. *Listen and be wise.*

Be wise? She almost turned to glare at the crow outside before remembering she was in a room full of people watching her every move.

Cam's directive echoed through her mind and she realized using a different tactic wasn't as difficult as she thought it would be. She only wished Nathan were here to see her playing nice with Kate.

Nathan. Her heart wrenched. She needed to find him.

"Have you heard from Nathan?" Eva and Kate both asked

each other at the same time. Kate's eyes widened, and an unfil-tered moment of confusion crossed her face.

"I'm worried. I can't find him," Eva admitted before biting her lip and staring at the milky swirl in her mug.

"Maybe he doesn't want to be found." The sadness in Kate's voice had Eva glancing up in surprise.

Eva reached back and gathered her hair in her fist. She twisted it. "I won't accept that." She couldn't. She released her hair and set her hands on the counter, drumming her fingertips against the cold plastic.

Kate's eyebrows rose. "You've been glued to his hip since the day you arrived in town. Why is that?"

Warning alarms blared inside Eva. Kate was fishing, but if she thought to use Eva's love for Nathan as bait, she had another thing coming.

"He needs someone who accepts him for who he is. Not for what he used to be." The people of Redemption needed to realize that before they destroyed him.

Kate snorted. "That man needs someone in his life who can guide him back to where he used to be, not lead him in a direc-tion that will destroy his soul."

The challenge she'd just been issued was palatable.

Game on.

At this moment, the directive from Cam meant squat. Nathan didn't need people in his life to change him, he just needed people to accept him.

Eva leaned forward and met Kate's glare head-on. "Living in the past is what is killing him. Why can't you see that? His life has been altered to a point where there is no going back. He's more than just a title. Reverend means nothing to him, not anymore." She swiveled in her seat. "The sooner you all accept that, the faster he can heal. If you loved him, really loved him, you would let him live life the way he needs to, not the way you expect him to."

She needed to get out of this cafe. Trying a new tactic was

like asking her to throw out her closet full of red scarves and wear white ones instead. Not gonna happen. Not in this lifetime or even in the next.

"Thanks for the cake and coffee. Let's do it again sometime."

She couldn't help the smile that grew across her face as Kate's eyes widened before she left the cafe.

She noticed the large black crow from earlier sitting on top of her bike. The crow lifted its beak as if nodding. Eva caught the flash of red on its chest. She would have sworn the bird winked at her.

"Well, that didn't go as planned," Eva muttered to the bird, which flapped its wings until it hovered just above the bike. She reached for her helmet and frowned. What the hell just happened in there? When Cam found out she'd just challenged the very people she was meant to win over, he'd rip a strip off of her.

Ever since the damn cacodaemon had come to town, nothing had gone right. Nathan was the only one who should have been affected by his turning. No one else. This town was supposed to have been protecting Nathan, who, in turn, protected the town. So what had gone wrong?

"Eva."

She peeked over her shoulder to find Kate standing at the door.

"Find him. Find my boy and bring him home. Please?"

She held out a white box in front of her. Eva glanced at the box and wondered what would be inside. It's not like Kate to hand out peace offerings so quickly.

Eva bit back a sarcastic reply when Kate said please. It wasn't the word, but how she said it. Broken. Hesitant. So instead, she nodded and held out her hand. When Kate stepped forward and handed her the box, Eva waited.

"It's the last piece. A man likes some curves on his woman. I'll have Jack start saving a plate for you at dinner time too."

Eva stood there, speechless. Dinner? Curves? As she looked

down at the box in her hand, a slow smile spread across her face, and a whisper of longing settled over her. It worked. It really worked. Kate only offered those plates to people she kept close. Her inner circle. The inner circle of Redemption.

A shiver of excitement ran through her body. She did it on her own. By being herself. Standing up to the people of Redemption and not backing down. She couldn't believe it.

Now all she needed to do was find Nathan and help him with the turning.

Damn it. Where the hell was he? He was in the midst of turning and had no bloody idea what was going on. If it happened without her there, there'd be hell to pay, and she'd be the one in debt.

A Nephilim needed his mate when he turned, to help ground him. Steady him. Keep him from going over the edge.

She'd stopped him one other time from doing just that, from going over the edge. If she didn't find him, there were no guarantees she could do it again.

Nephilim's home.

Eva stopped breathing. Nathan was home?

The crow cawed as it flapped its wings. It hovered directly over her bike. *Nephilim. Home. Now.*

Eva jumped on her bike and locked the cake box in the small compartment behind her seat. Nathan was home. Finally. Loose rocks skidded beneath her tires as she drove out of the parking lot and down the street.

It took only a few moments to realize that something was wrong. Eva cleared her suddenly dry throat. Something was very, very wrong.

If Nathan was home, why couldn't she sense him?

CHAPTER
TWENTY-EIGHT

NATHAN

Nothing had changed. Not the manicured bushes that looked a little too perfect, not the fresh smell of cut grass in the early morning dew. Not even the sparkling white facade of the Mount Joseph Private Hospital had changed. The gold sign remained untarnished.

Nathan remembered the first words out of his mother's mouth when they viewed the building. Ethereal.

What help could he possibly get by staring at the building that had torn his life apart? He knew the moment he'd stepped into the old house last night that he'd have to come here even if it meant breaking a promise.

Ever since Sue died, he'd been living in a bubble. As if life were waiting, anticipating what would happen next.

He'd never been one to wait. It hadn't bothered him -- until now. So what was different? He'd been content staying in Redemption, leaving only for the occasional trip into the city.

Rachel's death. That's what changed. The one person in his life, who was pure and honest. She didn't deserve to die. And that's when he realized he wouldn't let another person in his life be killed because of him.

Because if he were to be honest with himself, Rachel's death was his fault. Maybe not directly, but... She was dead because he couldn't face the truth of what was happening to him.

As of today, that was all about to change.

Nathan stepped off the sidewalk ledge and crossed the empty street. The park was covered with benches along stoned-lined pathways. He headed to the one that provided the best view of the only room he really cared about.

His mothers.

What was she doing? Was she still a morning person, eager to welcome the sun into her day? Was she sitting there, enjoy her hot cup of tea with a spoonful of honey? Or was she so heavily medicated that the sun rose without her welcoming smile?

A lone crow sat perched on a thick tree branch feet away from where he stood. Nathan ignored it. No matter where he went anymore, crows followed him. One, two, a murder.

When Eva had first told him that a flock of crows was called a murder, he'd laughed. Until he remembered the way the crows hovered over him when he stood beside Rachel's truck and held her dead body in his arms. The way they crowded him blocked out the moon with their black wings...being called a murder of crows fit.

A shudder ran over his body. He was never alone, never without the unwanted company of the demons.

And they were demons. He knew it. The way their eyes glowed, they could be nothing else.

They sure as hell weren't guardian angels, despite Eva's belief. Rachel would still be alive otherwise.

Nathan reached for the zipper of his leather jacket and lowered it. Despite the early morning hour, he was sweating. He stretched his shoulders and winced at the sharp jolt of pain that shot down to his tailbone. Something was wrong with him, but he wasn't sure what. One moment he'd be crippled in agony, and then the next moment, he'd have strength coursing through his body.

Fatigue swept over him. Sleep was a non-existent experience for him. The last time he'd had a good night's sleep was the night before Rachel died. Since then, nightmares plagued him the moment he closed his eyes.

He could still see her lying there against the steering wheel. He still felt the rain pelting him as he slid down the slope towards her truck; the sound of the relentless cawing of the damned crows still rang in his head.

Always the damned crows.

"Why can't you leave me alone?" He stared into the eyes of the crow as it flapped its wings.

Nephilim. Son of Morax.

Nathan hated those four words. They were seared into his brain, like a tattoo. No matter where he went, no matter what he did, they were there.

He reached inside his leather jacket and pulled out a crumpled piece of paper. He didn't need to open it to know what it said. He'd already read it a million times.

The penned words had torn his life apart, stripped him down to the depths of his soul without offering any hope, any recourse for redemption.

He was damned. The God he'd once preached about, worshipped, and adored had not only abandoned him but condemned him as well.

He'd been damned at the moment of conception.

A soft trill of laughter carried in the wind.

He counted to ten in his head before two female joggers passed the tree line on the far side of the park. He had about a half hour before the residents would come out for their early morning walks if he remembered correctly.

"Promise me you'll never come back here. Not to visit. Not to mourn. I'm dead. The moment you leave this room, I am dead. Other-

wise, it won't be safe. Not for you, not for me. Don't write. Don't call. Please, Nathan, please, leave me behind. While you still can."

He shouldn't have listened to her. He never should have promised. He didn't understand then, not like he did now. He'd thought it was the craziness, the unsettledness in her mind, that made her like that. He should have believed her when she whispered her fears, when she admitted what she saw.

But he'd promised.

Even though it broke him inside.

Every lie he told killed him. Especially when he'd had to lie to Sue.

That was the one mistake he would forever regret. Not trusting his wife enough to tell her the truth about his mother. If he had, she would still be alive with their child. Of that, he had no doubt. Their marriage might not have survived, but she would have.

He stared up at his mother's window on the second floor of the hospital and noticed the curtain move. Nathan leaned forward, his elbows resting on his knees. Was she standing there, staring out into the park? Did she see him? Did he want her to see him?

He had so many questions. There are so few answers. Her journals weren't enough. They would never be enough. He needed to see her, to talk to her. To be told the truth.

Nathan stood and placed the crumpled piece of paper back into the pocket of his jacket. Enough was enough. Too many people had already died because of a lie he lived to protect.

He couldn't do it anymore.

Eva's face flashed before him. He knew what Eva would say if she were here. She'd tell him to stop playing chicken. To live the life he was meant to live, not the life others forced upon him.

He took a step forward and stared up into the room. The curtains remained open. He could see the outline of a hand against the window pane. Was that her? He took another step.

The hand disappeared moments before the curtain closed. Against him.

The crow in the tree landed in front of him. Its wings flapped until it hovered in the air.

Home. Nephilim. Go home. Now is not the time.

"For what? There's nothing for me at home but graves. My life in Redemption is over."

A sharp sound burst out of the crow's beak. *New life begins in Redemption.*

A sudden wave of heat flowed through Nathan's body moments before his body felt like it was being torn in two. He dropped to his knees in agony while struggling to keep his lips clamped tight to contain the scream that rolled through him. His nostrils flared as he struggled to breathe through the pain. He counted to three, sure that the pain would cease as it had in the past, but it only gained momentum, ripping through his entire body until he thought he would burst into flames.

He was going to die.

CHAPTER
TWENTY-NINE

MORAX

It was hard to keep the smile off his face. Everything was coming along as planned.

"Please open the curtains, Morax."

He fingered the fabric in his hands, letting rays of sunshine filter through as he pulled it back.

"Your wish is my command." Triumph laced the tone of his words as he took in Nathan hunched over on the ground, clearly in excruciating pain.

It was happening.

The time of Nathan's rebirth was here.

A flicker of misgiving appeared, but Morax dismissed it. The pain could have been lessened if Eva had done her part. She chose to rebel, with Nathan paying the price.

Morax stepped to the side of the window and turned to stare down at Joanne Hanlin, the mother of his child.

Her frail body soaked up the morning rays as the light lingered over her face. She was as beautiful now as she had been all those years ago with her youthful vigor and innocent heart. He'd used her purity to his advantage, and it ended up being his weakness.

"What's caught your interest this morning, Morax? You rarely linger unless there is a reason." Joanne's head was tilted back in her seat, her eyes closed. She rarely looked at him anymore. Not since the day she'd woken up from her coma and realized who her doctor really was.

He rubbed his hands in glee. She thought she could outsmart him, ignore the reality of his presence. She was merely a pawn in his game.

"Only our son," he feigned indifference while he glanced one last time out the window to find Nathan now on his knees, his back arched as he struggled to regain his footing.

"Nathan?" Joanne gasped and bolted upright from her leaning position, grasping the handrails of her chair.

She stared at him, her eyes wide as she struggled to stand. Morax offered his hand to help her, but as usual, she ignored him.

"Tsk. Tsk. You don't always need to be so stubborn, my dear. One touch will not hurt you. In fact, it will heal you. When willingly received." He watched the struggle in her eyes to understand his words. He'd upped her dosage in the last few days, needing her to be weak in body. "Will you receive?" He repeated his question.

"And what healing would I receive at the hand of the one who condemned my soul?" Joanne rose to her feet, victory shining through her eyes as she straightened her shoulders to stand erect.

Morax smiled at her ignorance. "I didn't condemn your soul, Joanne." His hand dropped to his side as he turned back toward the window. "You did."

He heard her small gasp. Her feet shuffled as she approached the window.

"Why is he here? He promised me he would never come back." She leaned in toward the window, her hands gripped the small ledge for balance. Tears flowed down her cheeks as she gazed upon her son for the first time in years.

Morax gave her time to soak in the sight. Her tears tugged at his heart before he steeled himself. He could not afford any weakness. Not here. Not now. Especially not now.

Time was of the essence. His son needed protection as his body adapted to his true destiny. He'd give Eva one last chance.

"It's time, Joanne."

She whipped around, surprising him. "You will not do this to him." She shook as she stared at him. Her sudden burst of strength surprised him. Color flooded her skin, taking away the opaque look and replacing it with a healthy pink glow. Her fighting spirit had returned.

"It's out of my hands now." Morax held them up in a look of surrender. If only she knew.

"Liar." She spat. Apparently, she knew.

Morax unfurled his body from the slouching position he'd taken against the wall as Joanne gazed upon her son. He stood to his full height, allowing some of his majestic glory to be seen. With just one thought, he could have Joanne in rapture as she gazed upon him. He could have her madly in love with him. Again.

But, even after all this time, he wanted it to be her choice, just like before.

"You are asking me to unravel a lifetime of work." He'd give her the truth, even just this once. It might help in the coming days if she understood.

She shook her head before turning her attention back to the window. "What is a lifetime to you compared to the numbered days we live?" She whispered.

Morax stepped toward her until his body dwarfed hers. At his full height, her head barely made it to his chest. He remembered the feel of her hair on his skin as he held her close that one night so many years ago. The night when he knew he'd been saved. The night Nathan was conceived.

He placed his hands on her shoulders. "His days will soon be lengthened. His life...he will make a difference for others. This is only the beginning." Excitement flowed through him. He could almost taste the culmination of centuries of planning. It was intoxicating.

His eyes searched the hospital grounds until he found what he was looking for in the park. Finally.

Joanne turned and placed her hands on his chest. Her fingernails dug into his skin while the contact seared him. "Not many survive the turning. You yourself told me that."

He shrugged his shoulders. "And yet, here he is. Alive."

"Make sure he stays that way." Joanne pushed him away.

Morax took a step back but remained close. His focus was no longer on the woman in front of him or even on his son. Rather, he stared at the man he had once called brother and nodded. Yes. This was perfect. Even better than he'd anticipated.

"Oh, he will live. I guarantee it."

Nathan was no longer an unknown. A mere mortal to be ignored. From the moment of awakening when his body began its transformation, Nathan had caught the attention of those who knew his worth.

Like Morax's own angelic brother.

CHAPTER
THIRTY

NATHAN

Nathan struggled to his knees, the pain unbearable as he forced himself off the ground. As he breathed in deep, his nostrils flared, and his mouth thinned, but he fought past the pain and the urge to scream.

What was happening to him?

The moment he left Redemption, the pains had started. First, sharp shooting jolts of electricity traveled down his spine. His muscles would twitch, then burn as if on fire, while his insides felt like they were shredding into small strips.

He should go to the hospital.

But he wouldn't. He couldn't.

He braced his hands on his knees to heave himself up, but a hand grabbed his arm. Nathan glanced up and was dazzled by the bright light surrounding the man who stood before him.

"I'm dead, aren't I?" Nathan let the man pull him up to a standing position and followed him over to the bench he'd sat on earlier.

"Not if I can help it."

Nathan took a breath and realized it didn't hurt this time. So he took another one while straightening his back. The pain lessened. He caught a whiff of vanilla, faint but distinctively soothing. When the man sat down beside him, Nathan raised his head and realized it wasn't an angel who stood before him. The running shoes and drenched t-shirt gave it away. Another jogger.

"Thanks, I don't know what happened there."

The man nodded and extended his hand. Nathan shook it. A warm sensation tingled through his skin, up his arms. Within seconds the pain disappeared. Nathan released the stranger's hand and wiped his palm on his jeans.

What was going on?

"Feeling better?" A knowing smile lit across the man's face, but Nathan could see the genuine concern in his eyes.

"I do. Thanks again." Nathan went to stand up. The front doors to the private hospital were opening, and the last thing he wanted was to be seen by anyone.

He doubted he'd be recognized, but it wasn't the right time to see his mother face to face. Not now. Not yet.

The man's hand grabbed his arm. "Please, let me help you." He stood with Nathan and placed his arm around Nathan's back.

Nathan should have stepped away, insisting that he was fine and could walk on his own, but the comfort of the stranger's arm supporting him felt too good to pass up.

"Nathan." He introduced himself.

"Yeah, I've seen you here the past few days while on my runs. I'm Zeke." They followed the stone-laid pathway to the other side of the park where Nathan's vehicle sat.

The moment Zeke's arm lifted off of Nathan's back, an instant bolt of pain laced through him, ripping the muscles in his back to shreds. Again. Nathan gasped as he bunched over.

When Zeke opened the passenger door, it was all Nathan could do to crawl in. It took him a few moments to realize Zeke sat in the driver's seat and had found the keys he'd thrown on the floor.

"Let's take you home, shall we?"

"Hospital," he whispered to the man who now held his life in his hands. Images like he'd seen back in Redemption danced in front of his eyes. He swore he saw the slight outline of black wings whirl around his head, and their annoying caws filled his mind.

The pounding in his head increased along with the pain that shot up through him until he thought he was going to pass out.

He managed to push his legs out ahead of him and slouch into a somewhat comfortable position. Maybe it was time to stop ignoring what was happening to him. Maybe he really was dying.

Eva.

If he was dying, he wanted her here. With him. Why did he shut her out like he did at Rachel's funeral and afterward? He should have explained where he was going. She would have understood.

Zeke's warm fingers touched his arm. "You'll be fine soon. I promise."

Nathan closed his eyes. He believed him. Why, he wasn't too sure, but he believed him.

CHAPTER
THIRTY-ONE

WHEN NATHAN OPENED his eyes again, it was to see the old abandoned house he'd been sleeping at. His old home.

Zeke stood outside, holding the passenger door open for him.

"You just need some rest. Trust me."

Nathan leaned forward, expecting to be hit with another jolt of agony, but the pain was gone. He went to lift his legs out, but they were dead weight. They refused to move. And his arms felt like leaded rock as he tried to lift them.

Zeke chuckled. "Your body has suffered a lot. Get some sleep, and you'll feel like a new man tomorrow."

Nathan wanted to ask him how he knew and what he knew, but the thought of opening his mouth and forming words was too much. He'd never felt this tired before. It scared him.

The lone cry of a crow rang out on the empty street. Nathan glanced up at the porch and scowled. "They're always around."

Zeke turned and looked up. "Maybe they're watching over you." He stood to the side as Nathan forced himself out of the vehicle and set his feet down on the pavement.

With a sigh, Nathan allowed Zeke to help him across the street and up the steps to the porch. He turned at the door toward Zeke, fully intending to say goodbye, but there was a look on the man's face -- almost as if he knew what Nathan was going to do and wouldn't accept it. Which was very odd, considering they were strangers.

And yet, for some reason, Nathan felt like he'd known this man all his life.

It was Zeke who pushed the unlocked door open.

It was also Zeke who headed to the small kitchen and grabbed a bottle of water from the counter while Nathan sat on the ragged couch he'd turned into a bed and struggled to remove his shoes.

When he reached for the water Zeke held out, their hands connected and a jolt of electricity shot through Nathan, but instead of deep agony, a warm tingly sensation flowed through his veins.

"You're in shock. Don't ask me how I know, I just do. You've left the sanctuary that would have helped you through your transition." Zeke stepped back and headed to the door. His hand lingered on the knob before he opened it. "Return to it, and she can help you. I'll be close by. Just tell her Zeke is ready. She'll understand."

Before Nathan could say a word, the man he at first considered an angel, left.

CHAPTER
THIRTY-TWO

NATHAN DRANK the water and carefully placed it on the table before lying down. He couldn't stay upright for one second longer.

How did Zeke know where to take him? Nathan certainly didn't remember giving him an address, let alone directing him here.

There was something about the man, something he should know, but it was out of his reach.

Zeke's words played over in his head. Sanctuary. The one you need. She'll understand. What did he mean? How would he know?

Eva used to tell him Redemption was their sanctuary, the one place where they were safe and secure from the evil in the world.

When she would find him at Sue's graveside, she would hold his hand and whisper, "I'm your sanctuary". He knew she didn't think he heard, but he did and never questioned her about it. What would he say? He wasn't ready to delve into those emotions. Not then.

Was he now?

He had no idea. He only knew he missed her. There was an ache inside of him that he was slowly realizing she had filled. He would get a whiff of her scent, brown sugar, and vanilla all rolled into one, and he'd look around, expecting her to be near. It was crazy.

But he needed her. And that scared him like hell.

There was something about Zeke that reminded him of Eva. He just couldn't pinpoint what that would be.

Nathan closed his eyes and pictured her in his mind. She was on her bike, her red scarf wrapped around her neck and her raven black hair blowing behind her in the breeze.

A slow smile spread across his face. There wasn't anything about her he didn't like. She was sassy and honest to a fault, refusing to hold back any punches even if she should. And she didn't care what the people of Redemption thought of her.

That's probably what drew him the most to her. Her confidence. Not to mention her sex appeal. He fought against that a lot.

Why? She'd made it clear time and time again that she'd welcome any advances. That he was the only one she was interested in.

Actually, when he thought about it - he was really the only one she interacted with. He knew she felt cut off from the people he considered family - Kate and Jack, to name a few. She was always there for him - as if she knew his moods and when he needed her the most. He never saw her with anyone else.

So what was holding him back? She was the only thing left in his life that made sense.

He breathed in deeply. He knew it was only his wishful thinking, but he could smell her there, with him. If he imagined hard enough, would he open his eyes to find her sitting in the chair across from his bed, or even lying beside him on the bed, their bodies close?

No. He knew she wouldn't be. He'd left town determined to

face the present alone. He wanted answers and he was too afraid to have anyone, especially Eva, see him at his worst.

Maybe that had been a mistake. Maybe, out of everyone he knew, Eva was the one person he should have confided in and trusted his fears to. He was slowly realizing just how much he needed her.

He glanced around the small living area. He hated this house. He hated everything it stood for.

Ever since arriving, he'd only once gone into the bedroom off to the side. At first, he'd been too afraid to venture further. The flash of light he'd seen when he first arrived continued nightly, from his old bedroom. He didn't know what it was and he sure as hell wasn't ready to find out.

Last night, however, things changed. He didn't know what or how, but that fear had disappeared. The moment he saw the flashes he ran down the hallway and threw open his door.

And found nothing.

Just darkness.

He headed to his mother's old bedroom and retrieved an object he knew his mom had hidden beneath a wooden board under her bed. She'd shown it to him once, months before they'd moved. He'd caught her late one afternoon, sitting on the floor holding a metal box in her hand. She'd tried to hide it from him but he'd already seen it.

She'd told him it contained all her secrets. Secrets she didn't want anyone else to know. That's why she hid it. He'd told her he wanted his own secret box. He could still remember the sad smile on his mother's face. She told him he wasn't old enough to have his own secret box, but one day he would.

And now he did. Except his box was hers. His secrets were hers. His lies -- all hers.

A heavy shroud of lethargy covered him but he fought the temptation to fall asleep. Since Rachel's death, he'd been plagued with horrific nightmares. Blood. Flashes of lightning.

Screams. He always woke up in a sweat, his body tense as prepared for an attack. He never understood the dreams.

But as much as he fought, he couldn't win this battle.

Eva's face flashed before him, blood streaking down her cheeks as her mouth opened wide and a snake slithered out.

CHAPTER
THIRTY-THREE

EVA

Eva idled her bike at the top of Nathan's driveway and stared at Nathan's empty house.

She'd never seen it so dark before. Not even the porch light was on.

She stepped away from her bike, and the realization that Nathan was really gone slammed into her. Her knees buckled, but she steadied herself. She kept hoping, praying that he would return, that he wouldn't really leave. Not forever. But seeing his house dark and empty, she realized she'd never really faced the truth.

Nathan could possibly never come back home, and there was nothing she could do about it.

For the first time ever, she was scared. Scared for the future, for what could happen to her -- without Nathan in her life.

She was scared for Nathan, who had to be experiencing the change without her.

Morax had once described what the change was like to her.

She'd only been eight years old, but he'd made it vivid enough that she'd never forgotten nor forgiven him.

He'd taken her down to the river that ran through Redemption, and they'd stood at a bend. It was a beautiful spring day; the chirps of baby birds filled the air, and Eva stood hand in hand with her father. All was right in her little world.

Morax had always told her stories of the Nephilim, who they were, and why he'd created them. Why he'd created her.

She'd always known that she was to serve as the mate for the Nephilim savior. As a small child, Morax described it as being the Queen of the Nephilim, the one to rule side by side with the King. She'd never felt more loved than at those moments.

As they stood at the bank of the river, Eva asked how the boy she loved would grow to be a Nephilim. With a snap of his finger, a fish burst out of the river, its scales glowing.

Eva watched, mesmerized, as the fish opened its mouth moments before its bones and innards spewed out and wrapped around the scales. As the carcass fell back into the water, she screamed and raised her hands to cover her eyes, only to have her father grab her wrists and force her to watch.

Amidst the splashing water, a moth surfaced, its off-white wings beating the air as it rose. With another snap of his fingers, the moth transformed into a crow, its black feathers glistening in the sun. With a flap of its wings, the bird flew forward, landing on her father's shoulder.

"The transformation will be deadly Eva, if you are not there with him. If we had not been here to help that poor fish during its transformation, it would have remained a monster. But because we were here, it became a beautiful creation, a king of its kind. There are no other crows like this one, Eva."

Eva couldn't take her eyes off the bird. She was fascinated by what she'd just seen. She raised her hand and held it out, palm down. The bird had hopped from her father's shoulder down to her wrist. She could still feel the grip of its claws as it dug into her tender skin.

It took years for Eva to realize that if they had not been there, standing on that bank, the fish would never have had to experience the awful transformation that was forced on it.

Her father's logic was flawed.

Eva glanced down at the leather wristband she wore. It was now indented beyond repair. She really needed to buy another one. That crow still lived with her. The bird was free to roam but would never live in the wild. Morax had brought it home and had given it to Eva to train. Not only had she trained it, but she'd learned for it. Shadow had been her only friend growing up, until she met Nathan.

The bird now perched on top of the porch rail and stared at her. Shadow's black eyes normally showed little emotion, but Eva knew better.

Inside.

Eva shook her head. No way. It wasn't time to go inside, not with Nathan away. She wasn't ready.

The key to the Restorer is inside.

Eva pursed her lips. "You lied to me. What gives?" Her eyes narrowed as Shadow ducked his head before flying to the side door of Nathan's house.

Inside.

She shook her head and crossed her arms. "No. You told me Nathan was home. You lied. Why?" She kept her voice down in case any of the neighbours had their windows open.

Restorer. Inside. Now.

She took a deep breath. In. Out. In. Out. The damn crow was so stubborn.

Nathan was not home. Obviously, and there was no way in hell she was breaking into his house.

Cam would have a heyday if she did. Her low profile would be blown to shreds. He'd specifically requested that she never get herself arrested. A little B&E on her record wouldn't look good for the future Queen of the Nephilim.

She disagreed with Cam's opinion, though. She'd be labeled a badass which would suit her just fine.

Shadow squawked at her as he hopped about. She held out her arm, and he flew to rest on her wrist.

Inside.

"Why?" She hissed at the bird as she stepped toward the door.

Answers.

"And how am I supposed to get in?" She opened the screen door and placed her hand on the knob. She intended to rattle it to show Shadow it was locked, but to her surprise, the door swung open.

"You knew, didn't you?" She glanced down at the crow and shook her head. Shadow cawed once and flew to Eva's bike, perched on the bars as if he owned it.

Eva turned her attention back to Nathan's house, more specifically, his door. Why wouldn't it be locked? Did he leave it this way on purpose, or had someone else been here previously?

She didn't sense any evil about. She knew it couldn't be the cacodaemon or any other demons -- the house was so heavily guarded that they wouldn't be able to even step one foot onto his property.

So why was the door open?

She peered around the corner into the dark interior. She couldn't see anything, just black outlines of things she'd assumed would be furniture.

She should go in just to make sure everything was okay, right?

She glanced at the doorframe but couldn't see any markings to indicate someone had broken the lock, but just in case...it would be the right thing to do.

The caw of crows filled the night sky. Eva glanced up and

saw the circling birds above her. "Hello, my friends." Nathan was correct that they were always around. She made sure of that.

She took a step inside. A glow settled on top of her palm, a ball of pulsing energy that shone just enough to light her way, but not enough to fill the room. She hesitated, listening for a sound, any sound, but heard nothing. She relaxed her stance and glanced around the spotless kitchen. Nothing was out of place. Nothing to indicate a bachelor lifestyle or even a hasty retreat.

She continued until she reached a hallway. At the far end was a nightlight, its soft glow illuminating four doorways. Three were closed. She stopped at the first door on her left and stopped. There was a glow filtered through the bottom opening of the door. Someone must be inside.

When she opened the door, she gasped and stumbled backward.

CHAPTER
THIRTY-FOUR

"WHAT THE HELL are you doing here?" Eva flipped the switch on to illuminate the room.

Of all the people she would have expected to be here, Cam Bryant was the last person on her list.

"Same thing you are." He stood in the center of the room.

Eva rested her hip against the wall as she looked around. Other than a rocking chair in the corner and a box, it was empty.

"Why didn't I sense you?" She should have. She always could. Cam's energy reminded her of a red chili pepper. Smooth to touch but dangerous to bite. And Cam's bite was deadly.

Dressed in an all-black outfit, Cam shrugged his shoulder. "You're getting lazy."

"Really?" Eva straightened, her back stiff before cocking her brow.

She stepped toward him. "I don't think so." She flicked her finger and blasted a stream of energy at him. He stood there, unaffected. "You're masked."

His head dropped for a split second, but Eva didn't have time to step out of the way. "You're not."

A blazing stream of fire licked its way up her boots and

danced across her calves until it came to her knees. She twirled her hand, and the flame diminished.

"What was that for?" Anger bristled up inside her, and it took all her energy to contain it. Cam never used his power on her. Never.

"You're getting lazy. The covering over this town has cracked, and you haven't done a damn thing to fix it. And if you don't, there will be nothing left for Nathan to return to." His lips thinned as he stared at her, challenging her to deny the truth.

"I can't do it without Nathan."

He grunted. "You can. You just don't want to."

Before she could argue, a crash sounded down the hallway. Like glass shattering.

She turned on her heels, but Cam rushed past her, pushing her out of the way as he charged out of the room and stood in the hallway.

Eva reached out mentally, but there was nothing out there, just emptiness. She couldn't sense anything. Not even Shadow, whom she knew, must still be waiting outside.

"Something's wrong. I'm blocked." She crossed the room to stand behind Cam, keeping her voice low.

Cam cocked his head to the left, down toward the end of the hallway. Flashes of light filtered from under the door, a kaleidoscope of colors that announced the unexpected presence of an angel.

"Why? Why are they here?" She whispered in Cam's ear.

He shook his head. "Same reason you and I are." He took a step backward, away from the door.

There could only be one answer.

An icy chill crept over her body, freezing her heart as the realization of what this could mean hit her. Her knees buckled beneath her, and if it wasn't for Cam's arm snaking out to catch her, she would have fallen to the floor.

"It's happening, isn't it?"

Cam's head turned toward her, his gaze burrowing into her soul.

"They wouldn't be here otherwise."

Eva turned and ran down the hallway, away from the room where she knew she would meet her death.

If the angelic guard was here, then they knew about Nathan.

Once they saw her, they would know what she was, who she was. An abomination in their eyes. With one thought, she would cease to exist. The guard had one duty -- to protect the throne. They would know she was created to do the exact opposite.

She was created to destroy that throne.

Just one time, she would like someone to ask her what she wanted.

She reached the kitchen and grabbed the counter to steady herself. Her whole body shook. This couldn't be happening. Not now. Not while Nathan was still missing. The image of Shadow before his transformation filled her mind and she remembered the horror she felt as she watched the fish become a monster.

"You need to find Nathan. Now." Cam stood beside her, his voice lowered as he searched the room.

She shuddered. "I can't." She bowed over the counter, grief etching its way into her heart. She was powerless, and Nathan was dying, somewhere alone and without her. Her throat constricted as she fought against the overwhelming sadness that threatened to consume her. She'd let him down. It was all her fault. She wanted Nathan to fall in love with her on his own account, she wanted the transformation to occur naturally without her interference.

But her pride had killed the man she loved even more than her own life. Eva stumbled out of Nathan's house to her bike. Shadow was gone. He knew and blamed her for what was about to come. She didn't blame him. He was right. It was her fault.

She tugged her helmet on and revved up her bike just as Cam flew out the door and rushed toward her. She ignored him, turned her bike around, and roared out of Nathan's driveway, unconcerned about the noise.

All she cared about was gone. Destroyed. Because of her pride. Morax had warned her that this would happen. Shadow had urged her to not let it happen. In the end, she had ignored them both.

Now what? She was nothing without Nathan.

Eva drove mindlessly down the streets with no destination in mind, other than trying to outrun herself. She didn't know what to do, where to go, who to turn to. Nathan was all she had. All she wanted. All she needed. Without him...she couldn't imagine life without him in it.

She drove through downtown, ignoring the startled looks as she zipped past people walking hand in hand down the streets. She couldn't bear to look into the lighted windows of Kate's cafe, knowing she'd failed even her.

As she hit the town limits, she knew where she was going to go. She revved up her bike and sped by the Redemption sign, uncaring that she'd left what little protection she'd had. It no longer mattered.

Lights illuminated the road ahead of her as she rounded a corner, catching her unaware as she veered too far into the opposite lane. With the blare of lights beamed straight at her, and the wind blanketing her body, she was unprepared to hear Nathan's voice in her head, shouting her name.

Startled, her hand released the levers on the handlebars while at the same time leaning too far to the side. She tried to straighten, but the bike was angled too deep and ended up skidding across the road.

Eva had no time to brace herself as her body rolled along the pavement directly into the path of the vehicle.

CHAPTER
THIRTY-FIVE

JOANNE

The late evening rays gently kissed her face goodbye. Joanne held her eyes closed, not wanting to destroy the sated peace that enveloped her. There'd been so little peace in her life lately.

The last month she'd been living a nightmare she'd once thought she'd run away from. She should have known better. There was no running away from destiny.

She sat in her worn recliner, her slippered feet resting on the stool. A lone tear wove its way down her cheek.

She'd made so many mistakes in her life. If she could have done things differently, she would have.

Running away like she had didn't accomplish what she'd hoped it would.

Sheltering her son so he wouldn't be exposed to his true nature was probably her biggest mistake.

Instead of trying to force Nathan onto a path that would lead him away from who he was, she should have been honest with him from the very beginning. She could have equipped him to fight against what he was about to become.

She should never have tried to hide it from him.

Joanne thought about the other morning when she saw Nathan outside her window. For years she'd yearned for another look, to be able to touch him, hold him in his arms. She wanted to see that her sacrifice hadn't been in vain, that her son was strong and healthy and full of life instead of death.

Instead, what she got was to see her son on his knees, his back hunched over in agony. She would never forget that look on his face when he raised his gaze to her window. Her heart broke all over again for her son. He'd been so weighed down by anger and sorrow. The pain was evident in his eyes, in the tilt of his mouth, and the strain of his neck.

Her son was being tortured without any knowledge of why and it was all her fault.

The soft whoosh of her door being opened caught her attention. Joanne stiffened. Was Morax back to torment her again?

She refused to look at him, it was easier that way. Easier to ignore the swell of emotions that tempted to distract her. He knew all her weaknesses and had no qualms about using them to his advantage.

The light footsteps eased her mind, though. The way the rubber swept over the vinyl floor rather than thudded across it confirmed the identity of her guest.

"Joanne dear, why didn't you eat all your dinner? You're not eating enough lately." Shelly, her long-time nurse, asked as she opened the lid to the forgotten food tray.

A slight smile settled on Joanne's face as she turned to watch Shelly shake her head. "I don't have much of an appetite. I wonder if it could be the new medication I'm on?"

She'd first met Shelly the moment she entered Saint Joseph. At that time, Shelly had been a young woman, around Nathan's age. She'd been seated at the front desk answering the phones for the receptionist, who was on break. Joanne recognized the gentle soul within the young woman and immediately requested her to be her full-time nurse.

Shelly pulled up a metal chair and sat beside Joanne. She reached and placed her hand around Joanne's cold fists.

"Dr. Max already changed the dosage. There should be no side effects." Shelly opened up the notepad she held. "Maybe it's time to get another set of blood work done."

Joanne shook her head. "I'm really not up for another round of needles, Shelly. I'll make more of an effort. I promise." She leaned her head back against the chair and stared out the window. A few residents walked around the park.

"I was thinking we should start our early morning walks again."

Shelly's back straightened as she turned her attention from her notebook to Joanne. She leaned forward and patted Joanne's hand. "That's the best thing I've heard all day."

Joanne smiled. Up until last month, she made Shelly take her for a walk through the park every morning before the other patients were up and about. Joanne relished the quietness in the air and enjoyed listening to the birds wake one another.

It was the only time in the day all was quiet in her world, where the supernatural left her alone.

Since she'd woken up from her nightmare, she'd refused to leave her room.

For weeks she would keep the curtains closed, refusing to watch a new morning arrive. Morax would torment her day in and day out with his visits. She continually berated herself for not realizing who he truly was. She had loved her doctor and anticipated his visits even. He would poke his head in with a smile in the morning and then stop by as his rounds were completed. Some days, he would linger as they discussed books, news, and gardening.

She didn't understand the blinders over her eyes to his true identity. Her fists clenched as the self-loathing took root in her heart. A part of her wished she'd never opened her eyes that day when she heard his voice. That same part craved for the illusion once more. The heart was a wretched thing.

"You know you'll need your strength for your morning walk. Why don't I go grab you a new tray of food?" Shelly rose before Joanne could respond. She glanced over her shoulder and winked. Joanne smiled back. She couldn't help it.

Shelly was like a daughter to her. She was a gift from above.

"You have no idea." A deep voice filled with mirth broke the stillness.

Joanne turned in her chair to find Morax standing by her bed.

"Why are you here?" She returned her attention back out the window, forcing her gaze away from him. He wore a white lab over a dark silk grey shirt and black slacks. He stood there looking sexy as sin.

"Have you forgotten already?" He sat in the chair recently vacated by Shelly, and crossed his legs.

Joanne swallowed hard. Where was her strength? Her determination?

"Why continue with the facade?" The weariness in her voice was undeniable. She was tired. Tired of fighting Morax every step of the way, of worrying about Nathan...just plain tired.

Morax leaned close, resting his elbows on his knees, and reached for her hands. She should have pulled away, but she didn't. She couldn't.

"There is no facade, Joanne." His lowered voice sent shivers to dance over her skin. "Every time we sat here, sharing with one another...it was real." His grip tightened as his head dropped low. "Sitting here with you was the only time I could actually be...myself. Do you have any idea what that means to me?"

As hard as she fought it, little pieces of her heart she'd once glued back together broke again. She saw not only the doctor she'd foolishly fallen in love with over the years but the boy who had stolen her heart all those years ago as well. Except then, he hadn't been a man, much less a boy. He was an angel.

In disgrace. A fallen angel with a millennium of experience of seducing pure-hearted women.

"I'm not sure you even know who that person is anymore, Morax."

The stoop of his shoulder and the bow of his back spoke louder than any words could have.

Why the vulnerability? Why now?

With a heavy sigh, Morax released her hands and sat back in the chair. A look of uncertainty flitted across his face for a minuscule second before a shield of mental armor took its place.

Within moments, the vulnerable man transformed into the formidable being that he was created to be.

Joanne steeled herself.

"Have you wondered where your sight has gone, why the stillness around you?"

Joanne sighed. Noticed? It was hard not to. For once, she had felt normal. She didn't have to pretend not to see the supernatural around her.

"I assumed it was your doing."

His lips uncurled into a smile. "And you never thought to say thank you? I'm hurt."

"I doubt that. Why? Why would you take away something I've always known?"

Morax leaned forward, anticipation dancing in his eyes. "But, not something you'd always wanted, is it? I knew you would never ask."

Joanne bristled at that comment. "What right do you have to tell me what I did or did not want?"

His brow rose. "So you deny it then?"

She pursed her lips. No. She couldn't deny it. That time during her coma when Morax held her hostage, and she had her sight taken from her was the worst time of her life. Not only from the torture she experienced at his hands but also from the blindness.

"Would you want your immortality taken away from you without consent?"

Morax shuddered. "I've only sheltered you, my dear, not taken the gift away. I thought you would enjoy the reprieve." He stretched his arms out before linking them behind his head.

She would give him that. "Thank you." The reprieve had been nice. For the first time in her life, she didn't feel burdened with the heavy responsibility she'd always carried.

Morax stood, pushed back the chair, and gazed out the window, blocking her view. After a quick glance over his shoulder, he moved to the other side of the window and stared out.

"How is he?" Joanne barely managed to whisper the words through the clot in her throat. Just thinking of Nathan, of the pain he'd be in, choked her.

"Our son?" A smile slithered across his face as his eyes lit up. A shudder ran through Joanne's body. "The transformation is taking place with unexpected allies helping him. Guiding him. It's better than what I expected or even anticipated." He dropped his head backward, exposing his throat. "I have waited a long time for this day to come."

Here was the fallen angel right in front of her. Gone was any pretense of humanity, the facade he'd faithfully maintained when around her.

This was Morax. Her personal demon, one-time lover, and torturer.

He was her heaven and hell combined in one.

Exhaustion swept over her. She was too old to be playing games with her heart. Too tired for the energy they entailed. S he may only be in her fifties, but she felt closer to eighty, and she blamed the man in front of her for that.

"Do you honestly think you can do it? Go against God himself?" Years ago, after researching what the Nephilim really were, Joanne stumbled upon Morax's plan. He didn't want to just change the world or conquer it. He wanted to rewrite history.

"Do you believe me to be evil, Joanne?" Morax bent forward, his hands gripping the back of the chair he'd vacated.

Joanne shrugged her shoulder. "I don't think you are evil. I know. I've seen the evil in you. I've experienced it."

Visions of the torment she'd endured while in her coma swept across her mind. The nurses might all believe she'd only been dreaming, but Joanne had seen the bruises and felt the broken bones before they'd healed overnight. She knew better.

Morax shook his head. "You disappoint me. I thought you were able to see beyond the facade to the true man inside." As he straightened, Joanne caught the sadness in his eyes before it disappeared.

Confusion clouded her judgment. Was he honestly remorseful? Did he truly believe himself to be good? He was a fallen angel. Condemned by God. What good could possibly be left inside of him after centuries of being shunned?

"I thought you, of all people, would understand. But it was too much to expect. You, created from dust, returned to dust yet loved unconditionally despite the repeated mistakes you make. Whereas I, who have seen your creator, worshipped him, touched him, am condemned forever over one mistake. I wished I could have taken it back the moment it was decided. That exact moment. Do you have any idea how that feels?"

Morax paced the small confines of her room, his hands knotted together behind his back. "I've watched your kind, humans, throughout the centuries as they make the same mistakes over and over - trying to be God, yet despite their atrocities, despite the evil that corrodes them - your kind is still loved. All you need to do is ask for forgiveness. Not beg. Not plead. Not even demand. Just ask, and it's given to you."

He stood in front of her and stared. She watched the mirage of emotions filter through this gaze. The hatred. The agony. The confusion.

"I would give everything to be in your shoes. Everything. I

would do anything to turn back time and erase that one moment from history."

With one final glance out the window, Morax turned and walked out of her room as quietly as he had entered. Joanne raised herself up, her hands gripping the armrests of her chair to catch a glimpse of whatever had held Morax's interest.

But she could see nothing. There was nothing outside but a dusk-filled park covered with a murder of crows.

CHAPTER
THIRTY-SIX

EVA

Light blinded her as she lay on the ground, her arm raised over her face. Her whole body burned as if on fire. She blinked, searching the area for her bike but everything was hazy, almost as if she was blanketed under a dark mist.

She could barely make out the dark shape as it made its way toward her, increasing in size as well as proximity. Struggling to raise her head, she winced at the sharp pain in her neck.

"What do you think you were doing?" The dark figure bent close. Straining, she noticed the cowboy hat and knew right away who crouched down in front of her.

Cam Bryant.

"Nathan called out to me." Eva reached out for Cam's help. He ignored her hand and reached his arms around her back and knees and lifted her up. She rested her head against his arm and relaxed.

"When?" Each step Cam took jarred a muscle in Eva's body until she couldn't distinguish which part of her hurt more.

When they reached his pick-up truck, Eva grabbed the door

handle to the back and opened it. Cam nudged it the rest of the way with his elbow before leaning inside and setting her down on the seat.

"Just before I fell." She leaned her head back against the soft leather and moaned as she slowly stretched out. Everything hurt way too much.

"Just before you slid across ten feet of asphalt, you mean?" There was a gruffness to his voice she didn't like to hear.

"Yeah." She closed her eyes and recalled Nathan's voice. There was something about it that worried her. Scared her even.

"I need to find him, Cam." She bent forward only to have Cam's hand on her shoulder push her back.

He lifted one foot on the running board. "You aren't going anywhere."

Eva shook her head. He didn't understand. "He needs me. I could hear it in his voice."

Cam groaned. "Think about it. If you could hear him, it means he's close by. Maybe even on his way home." He half turned his body to look behind him. Eva stretched her neck to see what he was looking at. "Something is out there. I'll check on your bike and put it in the ditch. I'll call someone out to retrieve it on our way back to Redemption."

Eva's hand snaked out and she grabbed onto his arm. "We need to find him. He's hurt."

"Then he'd better get used to it." Cam shrugged off her hold and walked away, closing the door behind him.

She needed him to understand. Nathan was hurting. Possibly dying. It was her duty to be there with him, guiding him. If she couldn't make it in time and if he died...tears streaked down her face. She would never forgive herself. Never.

She leaned her head back against the seat rest and waited for Cam to return. His role in her life had always confused her. As a child, he was her honorary uncle. As a teenager, he became a confidant, a friend. Now as an adult, she recognized him for what he really was. Her protector. Her guardian.

To Cam, she came first before everything else. Even before Nathan. But how could she get him to realize that without Nathan, she wasn't worth protecting?

"Even without Nathan, you would still be our Queen." Cam's voice startled her. "Why can't you see that? The two of you are equal in this, no one is better than the other. Morax led you to believe that you were only a tool. He knew if you had an inkling of the power you possessed on your own, he wouldn't be able to control you."

Cam sat in the front seat of the truck, his body twisted so that he was facing her.

"I need to get you back under the protection of Redemption." He turned and started the truck.

As he turned around to face toward town, Eva leaned forward and laid her hand on his tensed-up shoulder. "We need to find Nathan."

He stiffened beneath her touch. "You don't get it, do you?"

She pulled back her hand and flexed her fingers. They were stiff and sore. She should have healed by now. "Get what?"

Cam sighed. "Eva--" A large boom filled the air moments before silvered forked tongues of lightning illuminated the sky in front of them.

She sat forward, ignoring the protests her body screamed, and gripped the edges of Cam's seat. "Did that...was that..." Flames shot into the air in the distance.

"Redemption? Yes." The truck increased in speed as they rushed toward town.

Apprehension flowed through her. "What is happening?" A red glow filled the air the closer they came. Her sanctuary was falling apart. Why?

"It's time," Cam swore. "It's time, Eva, and you won't open your damn eyes to what's at stake." His fist pounded the steering wheel. "Without the Restorer, the sanctuary of Redemption is gone. There is no protection. Don't you understand?"

Eva squeezed his shoulder again. "I do understand. It's why we need to find Nathan. Bring him home."

They'd just reached the first building that led into Redemption. Ahead flashing lights of the town's rescue vehicles blocked the roadway.

"The Restorer isn't just one entity. Why you believed that lie, I'll never understand. I've tried to tell you over and over again. Nathan isn't the only important one here." The truck lurched forward as he hit the brakes. People surged toward the truck, knowing Cam, their Sheriff was there.

Cam pushed open his door and stepped out. Seconds later, he yanked open the passenger door and reached out. Eva placed her hand in his, awareness sweeping away the cobwebs in her mind at his touch.

"You are the Restorer, Eva."

CHAPTER
THIRTY-SEVEN

EVA STEPPED out of the truck and surveyed the nightmare she found herself in. Cam's words had thrown her off balance. She was the Restorer? That wasn't possible. Nathan was. She was only his mate. His helper. The one to hold him up.

"Eva." Kate's voice carried in the wind.

She whipped her head around to find her. But it was impossible.

Thick, black smoke billowed in the air, encasing the townsfolk crowding the middle of the road. The fire department stood with their hoses, blanketing what Eva now realized to be a burning building with water.

Kate's cafe was engulfed in flames.

Eva walked forward, her path opening ahead of her as she focused on the building. First, there was the uprooting of the massive oak tree in the park last week, and now the cafe across from it was on fire. What was next? Why was this even happening? What happened to the town that promised safety?

Where was their sanctuary?

Eva heard Shadow's whisper in her mind, and she glanced up.

Danger. Restorer. Danger. The bird flew in circles off to the left, just over where the town's magnificent tree had once stood. Shadow wasn't alone, however; a murder of crows joined him.

Where? Where was the danger?

A hand gripped her arm, pulling at the scarf around her throat. She jerked away while at the same time tugging at the scarf. A quick glance down showed the scarf to be in tatters. It must have happened while she skidded on the road.

"I need you to take Kate back to her house. And stay there. Don't leave until I come for you." Cam dared her to disagree with him.

Kate swatted at his arm before crossing hers over her ample chest. "We're not going anywhere until everything is under control. Got that, Sheriff?"

Cam shook his head. "Kate, the fewer people around here, the easier it will be for my men to do their jobs. Besides, we don't know if there will be another strike."

Kate's brow rose. "Jack won't leave until he knows all is safe. And I won't be leavin' without my Jack."

Cam looked around. "Where is Jack?"

Kate pointed to her right. Eva's breath caught in her throat. Jack stood there, his hands fisted at his side while he watched his store dissolve before him in flames.

But that wasn't what caught her attention.

"Neither will Eva. Isn't that right, girl?" Kate nudged her, forcing Eva to tear her gaze away from Jack and look at her.

It was as if time slowed as she stared into Kate's eyes. Eva inhaled, her lungs filling with more than just air. There was also a determination and a strength that she hadn't had previously.

As she slowly exhaled, she knew what she needed to do. And when Kate nodded her head, it was as if she was giving her permission to do it.

Eva turned to Cam and grabbed his hand. "Let us help. If you won't let me go to Nathan, then you need me to stay here and help. This is my town, Sheriff." Eva straightened her shoulders. "Let me help protect it."

Eva waited for Cam to deny her, but all he did was nod and turn his focus back to the fire. That was it? She finally claimed the town as her own, not just as Nathan's, and all he did was nod.

It's about time. Cam stared at her as he whispered those words into her mind. Eva let out the breath she didn't realize she held. Cam rarely spoke to her like that. He once told her mind speech was a gift he refused to waste on someone who didn't deserve it.

Apparently, she deserved it now.

"Oh, and Sheriff?" Kate waited for Cam to look at her. "There won't be another strike. You and I both know that. They sent their message. We got it loud and clear." She sighed before raising her hand to her brow. "Come on, girl, Jack's over there. Let's go." She reached for Eva's hand and pulled her along. Eva caught the sharp intake Kate tried to hide.

"Kate --" Eva started.

"No. Not one word, do you hear? I'll cry my tears later. It can be rebuilt. What I'm worried about is what's happening to our town. Things aren't right. Redemption is a sanctuary, not a prison of fear. Things have gone too far." Kate's lips thinned into a straight white line.

When they reached Jack, they stood as sentries on duty, side by side, without a word spoken between them. Eva caught the way Jack threaded his fingers through Kate's and squeezed.

A lump formed in Eva's throat. That's what she wanted. A partner in life to hold her hand when things got rough. A partner like Nathan. Except he wasn't here and she couldn't go find him.

"What happened to you?" Jack said, breaking the silence. "You look like you've been run over by a truck and barely survived."

Eva sighed. She couldn't look that bad. But then, she knew she didn't look like her glamorous self either. She reached back and fixed her hair, twisting the long strands into a braid.

"If I told you I heard Nathan call my name while I was riding my bike to find him, would you believe me?"

Kate snorted. "If we said yes, would you consider us crazy?"

Eva spoke the first thing that popped into her head. "Yes."

"Stranger things have happened. Like having a demon stand behind you as a guard."

Eva whipped around.

The cacodaemon stood twenty feet behind her. The cowboy hat the demon wore hid its face, but Eva had no doubt that it was staring straight at her. Its black trench coat flapped in the wind, and a dark cloud swirled at its feet.

What are you doing here?

The cacodaemon didn't respond. She glanced over her shoulder and realized both Jack and Kate now watched her instead of the fire.

Why can they see you? Kate stepped forward to confront the demon, only to stop when it stepped back and sank down to one knee.

Many things are kept hidden until the day of revealing. Restorer.

"Get up." Kate gritted her teeth while clenching her hands. This was happening too fast. Too soon. She needed Nathan here, by her side. Damn it.

Loud caws filled the air, their loud noise overpowering the town folks' cries of alarm as a swarm of crows filled the park, and people moved out of their way as the birds settled on the ground around the cacodaemon.

Welcome home.

Shadow hovered in the air in front of Eva. She raised her arm out and welcomed the heaviness of her friend as it settled on her arm. When Shadow bent his head down, it took Eva a moment to realize what was happening.

Her heart raced as she glanced around her. She forgot about the roar of the fire behind her. She ignored the panicked cries of the people who watched her. All she focused on were the bent head of the crows before her and the hand on her shoulder as Jack stepped forward and stood at her side.

"It's too soon. It's not time." She whispered. Her nostrils flared as she struggled past the panic attack that was about to overwhelm her.

"Peace, child," Kate's voice whispered into her ear as she grabbed Kate's hand.

Eva turned to Kate and noticed the multicolored streams of light emanating from her, the same as she'd seen from Jack earlier as he stood watching the fire. Jack and Kate were of the angelic guard. Why they were here, now, at this time -- Eva had no idea.

"The Restorer is the bridge for those who made a mistake that can never be undone." Jack's grip on her shoulder tightened.

Eva turned to stare at him. "You are a Guardian." At Jack's nod, Eva tore her hand away from Kate's and stepped back. "I don't understand?"

She wanted to run. None of this made sense to her. Guardians were those who chose to ensure the destruction of the protector. They were the ones who killed the Nephilim.

"That's where you are mistaken, child." Kate's voice calmed the swell of confusion that surrounded Eva.

"There are only ever two Guardians for each Nephilim. Their role is to help guard their charge before they begin their transformation. It's not the Guardians who destroy the Nephilim before they are fully reborn."

Eva shook her head. That didn't make sense. Morax had always warned her about the Guardians, he'd taught her that they were the enemy.

"So, you're here to protect Nathan?"

Jack shook his head. "We are the caretakers of Redemption. That is our primary goal." He reached for Kate, who moved to stand beside him.

Kate placed her arm around Jack and rested her head for a

brief moment on his shoulder. "Redemption is your shelter, child. It was created to protect both you and Nathan." She shook her head and glanced around at the crowd surrounding them. "We're not the only Guardians here, Eva."

Eva tore her gaze away from Jack and Kate and searched the grounds for Cam, ignoring the people who crowded around her. She realized the crows and the cacodaemon had disappeared.

Eva balled her fists together. Energy flowed through her veins, and she struggled to understand what was happening, except she couldn't. None of this made any sense to her.

Nathan's energy trickled into Eva's awareness, and she sensed his confusion and something else. Fear.

"If the Guardians aren't the ones who are out to destroy Nathan, then who is?"

CHAPTER
THIRTY-EIGHT

JOANNE

Joanne's internal alarm clock went off. She couldn't stop the smile from spreading across her face as she sat on the edge of her bed and slipped her feet into her slippers.

Something was going to happen today. She could feel it in her bones.

There was a soft knock on her bedroom door moments before Shelly popped her head in. "Ready in five?"

Joanne raised herself from the bed and shuffled across the floor. "I might need a few more moments. These old legs of mine don't seem to be working like they used to."

Shelly smiled. "They're just out of practice. All you've done is sit in your chair for weeks now." She left just as quietly as she came in.

As Joanne got ready, she realized there was something about Shelly today that she'd never noticed before. A soft white glow surrounded her. A glow she normally only saw when an angelic presence was around, which was odd since she'd never noticed it before.

Or maybe it was the light from the hallway, and Joanne's sight was getting really bad.

By the time she was ready for her walk, Shelly was waiting for her with a cup of tea in a travel mug. Joanne locked arms with the darling girl as they made their way down the hall.

"I can't tell you how happy I am that you are walking again." Shelly smiled down at her, her eyes alit with warmth.

Joanne patted her hand. "Did you talk to the doctor about my dosage? I feel different today. Better."

Shelly shook her head. "That's not the issue, Joanne. It's time you let go of the fear that has been holding you hostage the last few weeks."

Joanne stared straight ahead. "I don't know what you're talking about."

Shelly stood still, forcing Joanne to do the same. They were in the middle of the hallway, three feet away from the main doors that would take them out of this wing and into the main hospital area.

"Of course you do. After the torment you went through during your coma, you've held onto the fear. Your eyes are closed, Joanne. You need to open them. It's time to see the truth."

Joanne searched her nurse's eyes for a hidden meaning. "You mean face the truth, don't you?" Of course, that's what she meant. She didn't know that Joanne could see into the spirit realm. No one knew. She'd kept that secret guarded close to her heart.

Shelly reached out and laid her palms on Joanne's cheeks. A heat radiated from her skin. She closed her eyes as Shelly's fingers gently swept over her eyelids. "See, Joanne. See the world through the eyes of the one who gave you this gift."

Joanne slowly opened her eyes and marveled at the bright glow emanating from the woman beside her.

"I don't understand," she whispered, confusion over-whelming her. If Shelly was an angel, how--

"He's not as bad as you think he is." Shelly's hands dropped until they gripped Joanne's. "There's goodness inside, just hidden beneath the layers of hurt and anger."

Joanne shook her head. Her stomach coiled with tension as she thought about Shelly's words. None of this made any sense to her. "How can you say that? Knowing what he is--"

"An angel who made a mistake." She shrugged her shoulder. "They aren't all bad, just...condemned." There was sadness in her voice that surprised Joanne. Shelly threaded her arm through Joanne's and took a step forward.

"Most of them spend an eternity being reminded of their sin, while you long for the opportunity where you can forget them."

Joanne's confusion must have been evident on her face. The shadow that lingered in Shelly's eyes didn't disappear.

"Think of it this way, Joanne. Every family argues. Just because they're related doesn't mean they all have to travel the same path or agree on the same things. But in the end, no matter what, they are still family. That will never change."

The door to the outer room was directly in front of them. Shelly laid her fingers along the handle and gripped it before winking at Joanne.

"Ready?"

With a deep breath, Joanne straightened her back. Energy coursed through her, and excitement built up. There was something about this day, something she knew she needed to hold onto.

As they walked into the main foyer, the soft light of dawn filtered through the large windows. Peace resonated within her as she tightened her grip on Shelly's arm. She looked out the corner of her eye at the woman, who was really an angel. She shook her head. She, who could see all things natural and supernatural, had been so blind.

Either that or she wasn't to have known. But it didn't matter. Not anymore. Because if her nurse was really an angel, then it meant God had not abandoned her as she thought.

A warmth filled her soul. No, God was still there. Loving her. Caring for her. Forgiving her.

Shelly turned her head and smiled down, her gaze meeting Joanne's.

Yes, she was forgiven. And loved.

What about her son? The son of a fallen angel who was not forgiven and never would be? Where did he fit?

CHAPTER
THIRTY-NINE

NATHAN

Nathan drummed his fingers on the steering wheel as he sat in his Jeep. The box he'd brought with him was on his passenger seat once again; this time, though, it contained his mother's old secret box along with more journals he'd found this morning in her closet.

He brought the journals with him for his mother. He was determined to go see her. Even if it meant breaking his promise.

He didn't need to search for answers anymore. All the answers he needed were right in front of him. How he knew that, he wasn't sure. Yet everything inside of him screamed it.

Nathan stepped out of his Jeep and headed toward the park. The sun was just rising above the horizon, its pale orange and blue highlights illuminating the dark sky. The birds were quiet, still slumbering in their nests. A sense of peace surrounded him as he made his way along the pathway.

There was someone sitting on the park bench. The man's head was bowed and his shoulders hunched, but Nathan knew right away who it was. He knew the moment he'd pulled up. Zeke. His guardian angel.

"Good morning, Nathan," Zeke called out moments before Nathan rounded the bench to stand in front of him. Nathan glanced down and found a crow sitting beside Zeke. He shuddered. He really hated those birds.

"You may go now. But keep watch," Zeke lifted his finger and pointed to a tree directly across from the bench. The black bird cawed and then flew off toward that tree. It landed on a sturdy branch and sat, staring at them as if on guard.

"Who are you?" Nathan sat down on the bench beside Zeke.

Zeke stretched out his legs and smiled. "You already know who I am."

Nathan shook his head. "No. I think I know who you are, but I would like you to confirm it." Nathan's back remained straight and stiff as he looked at the hospital. A soft glow lit up his mother's room. He couldn't help but smile. She always was an early riser.

"Why don't you like the crows, Nathan?" Zeke's soft voice broke the early morning silence.

Nathan shrugged. "Lately, they always seem to be around, especially when something bad is about to happen." He didn't understand why he admitted that.

Zeke turned and laid his arm along the back of the bench. "Perhaps they are there to warn you."

Nathan searched the man's gaze. There was nothing there to read but honesty. "They're birds. Not angels."

Zeke's brow rose. "Does that matter?" He waved his hand, and suddenly, the trees were all full of black crows, their feathers glistening in the early morning sun as it rose.

Nathan stared at the birds and waited for the unease he normally experienced to occur when he saw them. But there was nothing. They all just stared at him with their freakish, beady little eyes, as if waiting for him to make a move.

Well, they could wait there all day for as long as he was concerned.

"You tell me." Nathan ignored the birds and their sudden chatter and checked the time on his wristwatch. Today was the day. If his mother didn't come out for her early morning walk, he was going in to see her.

Then he was heading home. Home. To Eva.

"You seem to be feeling better today."

Nathan nodded. "Like a new man."

He woke up this morning feeling as if he were a different person. Gone were the aches and pains, the sharp stabs and torn muscles. He'd even gone for a run this morning, something he hadn't been able to do for a few weeks. The muscles along his chest and arms were more defined, harder even. He almost didn't recognize himself.

"Ready to conquer the world?" Zeke slowly straightened, drawing his legs inward and dropping his hands down to the seat of the bench. Tension filled the air as Nathan noticed Zeke's tight grip on the wood slats of the bench seat.

"If I need to." With the way he was feeling, he had no doubt he could. After all, isn't that what he was created for?

A crow flew toward Nathan, its body sleek as it glided down toward him. It hovered in the air above him.

Nephilim. Take care. Be ready.

"I am ready." Nathan shook his head when he realized he'd said that out loud.

Zeke chuckled beside him. "Talking to the birds now, are we?"

Nathan shrugged. "It spoke first."

There were so many things he'd learned through reading Joanne's journals. His abilities. His gifts. What he could do and what she thought he'd be able to do. His mother knew him better than anyone else. Even better than the one who made him.

It was the last line she'd written in one of her journals though, that would never leave him.

"My son will become a man no one can control but God alone. His purpose is greater than anyone can anticipate."

This is when his world rocked.

From the night when Rachel died, and he discovered what he was, he'd felt empty. Scared at the thought that everything he'd believed in, everything he'd held dear, had been pointless. He knew who the Nephilim were, and he knew, or at least he thought, that his soul was condemned.

But he'd forgotten one important key factor. He was still a child of God, created by God, destined by God. He wasn't alone. There was a greater purpose for his life, and he refused to sit by and just wait for life to happen to him.

The man he became after Sue died...that man disappeared last night. He wasn't just a cast-off created by a maniac. God knew him by name, his heart. God owned his soul. No one else.

"Now you are ready." Zeke's quiet words confirmed what Nathan knew in his spirit.

"What are you?" Nathan asked. He looked him in the eye and waited. The questions, the doubts, and the resolution that Nathan read in Zeke's gaze surprised him.

"I'm your friend."

Nathan nodded. It would have to do. He had a feeling if it hadn't been for Zeke coming to his aid yesterday, he wouldn't have survived whatever was happening. His mother called it a transformation. But from what he'd read, Nathan knew he should have died.

"Thank you." Nothing else needed to be said. He knew Zeke understood, he could tell by the way he lowered his head in reply.

He turned his attention back to his mother's window and was surprised to find it dark. If the light was off, it meant only one thing. She was no longer in her room.

He stood up and smoothed down his jeans before leaning

down to pick up the...he'd forgotten the box with his mother's journals in his Jeep. "I'll be right back."

A gust of wind swept in front of him. He thought he heard Zeke say something as he jogged away, but Nathan ignored him. There was no one around, and if his mother was coming out for her morning walk, he wanted to be ready for her.

His palms were sweaty at the thought. It had been so long since he'd last spoken with her. Too long. His throat clogged. All he wanted to do was give his mother a hug. Nothing else. No questions. No demands for answers. Just a hug.

Feet away from his Jeep, Nathan noticed that the temperature had dropped. His breath came out as puffs of white steam, and a chill ran down his spine.

Danger!

A crow sat on top of his Jeep, staring at him with its black beady eyes. Nathan pursed his lips but ignored the bird. He yanked open the door and leaned forward to grab hold of the box. He could feel eyes staring at him. He jerked when he saw someone standing outside his passenger door, looking in.

The guy was huge. At least three times Nathan's size with muscles the size of Fort Knox. He wore all black, but every inch of visible skin was tattooed. There was something...evil about him. The man peered down into the jeep and sneered at Nathan.

In that instant, Nathan knew he was a dead man.

Beware, Nephilim, Son of Morax.

Nathan jerked, and the man disappeared. He spun on his heels and searched the area, but there was nothing. No one.

A loud clap of thunder shook the area as Nathan raced down the pathway with the box in hand. Three crows flew around Zeke, who now stood in the middle of the park, his hand outstretched.

"We need to leave."

Nathan stopped. "No." He wasn't going to run anymore. He

ran from Redemption because he'd been too afraid to face the truth.

Well, the truth was right in front of him now, and there was nowhere left to run.

It was time to face it like the man he was.

Like the Nephilim he was created to be.

Behind Zeke's shoulder, Nathan noticed the doors to St. Joseph opening. "There's someone I need to speak with first."

The air rumbled as the wind swirled around them. Nathan stepped past

Zeke grabbed hold of Nathan's arm and squeezed. "There's no time."

A loud, piercing scream echoed throughout the park.

Nathan glanced up in time to see a dark cloud descend upon him. It reminded him of the cloud he saw in his backyard before Rachel's death. The center of the cloud contained swirls of silver and red, while black wisps of something similar to smoke but more dense, descended.

Nathan raised his arms to shield himself before everything went black.

CHAPTER
FORTY

MORAX

It was time.

At the snap of his finger he could end it all it. But he wouldn't.

No, Morax knew he would never be able to end it. Not when there was a remote chance that everything he'd worked so hard for, would come to pass.

From the moment of the fall, Morax knew that it would take a bold move to undo the past, to stop the present and be returned to his rightful place.

And if there was anything Morax was known for, it was his bold moves.

He wished Joanne could have believed in him. He'd waited patiently, even attempting to woo her again, but she would never forgive him. The mental anguish she'd experienced during her coma had destroyed any hope of that.

What she didn't know was that his hand had been forced. It was either prove his loyalty or have the woman he loved killed.

Losing Joanne wasn't an option, but then neither was losing his son.

Morax stood at his window's office and watched the scene below play out before him. Shelly promised she'd have Joanne out today, in time to meet Nathan before he returned to Redemption. He'd survived the first part of the transformation, thanks to Zeke stepping in. But he couldn't complete it without Eva. Morax had made sure of that when he created her.

She was all things perfection. Eva was created for one purpose in mind, and it didn't matter how much she fought against it; there was nothing she could do to change it. Free will was only allowed for humans.

Morax rested his forearms against the casing around the window and leaned forward. Nathan was running away from Zeke. Why? He caught the shake of Zeke's head before he stood up and followed Nathan down the path.

It was difficult to watch the scene being played out. Black-winged crows swooped out of the air and landed in the park's tree branches. He could hear their deafening caw from up here on the top floor of St. Joseph. A gust of wind shook against his window pane.

Those who say you can't see the way the wind moves obviously never looked at it through the eyes of the supernatural.

The wind was never colorless nor without a purpose. It could be seductive as it whispered across the skin of a beautiful woman, childish as it kicked up leaves for others to play in, or murderous as it swept over the land and sea, intending to destroy anyone in its path.

This was black. Evil. Whispered strands trailed to the side and behind the core flow.

Crows caught in its path died instantly, the pathways littered with dead bodies.

Morax anxiously followed the path of the currents as it headed towards Nathan.

Before it could reach his son, he called out, and in an instant, four cacodaemons he'd had stationed on the corners of the park surrounded Nathan.

The murderous air flow swirled around his beings but they held guard, protecting Nathan until he could reach the safety net that Zeke contained.

Time stood still as Zeke reached out to grab Nathan's arm, but Nathan sidestepped him. Morax groaned. He knew why. He felt her presence. Joanne was there.

Morax blinked himself out of his office down to where Joanne stood, just slightly behind her. He needed to get her out of there, to protect her from whatever was about to happen. Just as he was about to reach out to grab hold of her arm, Joanne screamed.

The evil force had managed to bypass his cacodemons and swirled around Nathan, knocking Zeke and the box Nathan held in his hands to the ground. The caws of the crows filled the air with a screeching pierce as they shouted in warning.

Within moments, a seething tornado stood in the middle of the park, its black mass doubling in size as the tendrils wrapped itself in its midst. It rose, towering over the trees and engulfing them, throwing branches and debris through the air.

Morax flung up a wall of protection and grimaced at the lifeless birds as they dropped to his feet. Shelly had thrown Joanne to the ground, her body covering her charge. With Morax beside her, Shelly's powers were limited, a pact made years ago that they'd used to their advantage.

Until now.

Frustration knotted inside Morax. He'd failed to anticipate this move of his enemy. He'd failed to consider all the threats, all the resources. He'd forgotten about the pawns left on the chess board in the game he'd started years ago, with the one person who could defeat him, if given the chance.

A scream ripped through the air, filled with anguish, despair, and pain. A lot of pain. The sound could only mean one thing.

A hand grabbed his fist and pulled.

Morax slid his gaze from the whirlwind that disintegrated before his eyes down to Shelly. Tears streaked across her cheeks as she cradled Joanne in her arms.

"She's dead." Heartache filled her voice as she gazed down at the woman she'd taken care of for the past few years.

Morax shook his head. "No." He choked and almost fell to his knees. His heart tore apart as he watched Joanne's lifeless body in Shelly's arms. He found himself breathing and waiting for her chest to rise. For so long, he'd matched his breath to hers, his heartbeat to her rhythm. She couldn't be dead.

They promised to leave her alone. They lied.

Shelly gathered her legs beneath her and stood, carrying Joanne in her arms as she did so.

He gazed down at the shell of the woman he'd fallen in love with when she was but a child. He'd watched her grow, sheltered her from the gift she'd been given, as much as possible while also teaching her to accept it. He'd spent years molding her into the woman he needed her to be.

He wouldn't accept her death. He couldn't.

"I need her." As he said the words he realized he truly did need her. She was his life. His purpose and his reason.

He reached out his arms, struggling to keep his voice calm, but knowing Shelly heard the scratchiness to his voice. The weight he now carried in his arms equaled the heaviness he felt in his heart.

Anger took seed in his heart, blackening it beyond recognition. If Joanne was dead, then he had no reason to continue on his path to redemption.

"Morax!"

Zeke's voice carried across from the park. He'd risen. Morax held Joanne close to his chest before he turned to find his caco-daemon surrounding the angel.

"You know what you need to do," Zeke called out moments before he walked away and vanished.

One day Morax intended to have a talk with his brother. One day.

Morax gazed down on Joanne's serene face. His heart hitched as he took in her essence. Even in death, she was beautiful.

Shelly stood beside him. "Take her to the sanctuary." She passed her hands over Joanne's body. "This is an unholy death." Tears welled up in her eyes.

"Are you sure?" Morax needed to know. If there was a chance she would survive--.

Shelly nodded. "Her soul still resides within her. Under that protection, she will revive."

Morax stared where Shelly's hand hovered. A mist of black fog hovered in the space between her hand and Joanne's chest. He'd seen this before. Many years ago.

"Will you come?" He knew her answer, but he needed to hear it.

Shelly's brow rose. "You know my power there will be stronger than yours."

Morax shrugged. There was a reason he'd left Redemption when he did. The caretakers couldn't fulfill their duties in the way he needed them to with him around.

Another part of the pact.

"You are still her Guardian."

Shelly shook her head. "I am her protector while she is here. Not in Redemption."

Morax gritted his teeth. He'd been betrayed once. It wasn't going to happen again. "I need you in Redemption. Allowances will be made." He'd make sure they were.

Shelly sighed. He knew the minute she admitted defeat. "It has been a long time since I last saw my sister."

A choice had to be made. Go after his son or save this woman.

There was only one solution.

Morax. We await.

Morax gritted his teeth as power flowed through him at the words spoken. How dare they summon him now, like this.

He bent his head down to lay a kiss against Joanne's cold lips and breathed his essence into her own. He saw her chest rise as his power flowed through her body. If he could, he'd will her heart to be with all the power he contained. But he couldn't.

Shelly laid her hand on Joanne's arm and looked him in the eye.

The choice had been made.

PART THREE
THE ORIGINAL

MORAX

CHAPTER
FORTY-ONE

SHELLY

Shelly wasn't sure what she expected when she returned to the home she'd left so many years ago, but this wasn't it. A town that used to radiate with warmth now forced a chill to snake its way down your spine.

She caught the gaze of several of those she knew from a life-time ago and nodded as she slowly drove through the streets until she pulled up into the driveway of her sister's home.

She didn't expect her homecoming to be quite like this.

The thrill of power welled up inside her and it was all she could do not to weep with joy. Here, the limitations to what she could do disappeared.

She'd warned Morax she'd be stronger here. She hoped he realized what that meant.

She watched the sleeping form of her charge in the backseat and prayed for a miracle but knew in her heart it wouldn't be that easy. The protection here wasn't as strong as she'd hoped it would be.

Something had happened in this town, to this town.

She honked her horn and waited for the curtains to flutter in the windows.

I'm home.

A smile blossomed on her face as her sister's face peeked through the curtains. It'd been so long since she last saw her family. A sense of peace rested upon her in that moment, knowing she'd done the right thing.

She got out of her vehicle and made her way up the driveway and into her sister's waiting arms.

"Now my heart is finally full. You've come home!" Kate's arms tightened around her.

Shelly hugged her back and squeezed. She almost didn't want to let go. She hadn't realized just how lonely she'd been for so many years without her family around her.

She'd known that this was the life of a Guardian, but at the time when she'd accepted her charge, the realization of what that heavy weight entailed never fully hit her.

"I've missed you so," Shelly whispered into Kate's ear.

"Well now, look who's come back home!" Jack's voice boomed from the front door. "Stop givin' our neighbors something to talk about and come inside. You're just in time for dinner."

"It's almost like he knew you were coming 'cause he made your favorite too," Kate wound her arm through Shelly's and started to pull her forward, but Kate stopped her.

"Joanne is with me."

Kate's face blanched for a moment as she stared into Shelly's eyes.

"I had no choice."

Kate shook her head. "Of course you didn't. Something must have happened. I should have expected that. Is there still time?"

"Morax believes so."

Kate spat on the ground at the mention of his name. Shelly laid her hand on her sister's arm and frowned.

"That was rude, even for you. You know better than that."

Kate's eyes narrowed. "This is all his fault."

"No." Nothing could be further from the truth. "It's all our fault. You can't lay blame on one angel, fallen or otherwise. One decision made centuries ago brought us to this place."

Kate shook her head, her gaze turning towards the sky. "My heart hurts over all this, you know that." She said.

Shelly knew. She could see it in her sisters' eyes and hear it in her voice. She was hurting.

"Help me bring her in? There was nowhere else to take her." Shelly opened the backseat door and leaned in. She wrapped her arms around Joanne's thin body and held her close as she pulled her from the vehicle.

She heard Kate's audible gasp but ignored it. There would be plenty of time for explanations later. For now, she needed her charge to be safe and protected, and there was no better place than in the home of the Guardians of Redemption.

"You were supposed to protect her." Jack's voice held the hint of accusation and was filled with despair as he took Joanne from Shelly's arms.

Shelly followed Jack towards the back of the house where their spare bedroom was located. Nothing had changed in the room since she last stayed there. The same frayed carpet covered the floor, the same shaggy pillow sat in the corner of the single bed along with the same lamp with what used to be a baby blue shade.

"You don't mind taking the couch?" Kate asked.

Shelly shook her head. Of course, she didn't mind.

"How long has she been like this?" Jack's voice crackled as he tucked the blankets around Joanne's thin frame.

"Since yesterday."

Jack's lips thinned into a straight line as stomped past Shelly and headed out of the room. Kate shook her head but followed behind her husband without a word.

Alone with Joanne, Shelly sat down on the side of the bed

and reached for Joanne's slightly warm hand. There was still hope, still time to set right that which was so very wrong.

She didn't look forward to facing Jack's wrath when she had to explain her actions nor did she think things were going to go well when she shared what happened with Morax and why she allowed things to progress the way they did.

But there was still hope and that's what mattered.

Shelly leaned down and breathed a prayer into Joanne's ear, a prayer of healing and love. She loved her charge more than she should and she knew that one day it might be the downfall of both of them. She only hoped that today wasn't that day.

CHAPTER
FORTY-TWO

MORAX

If there was one thing Morax did not like, it was being cornered.

Everything he'd done had been with one purpose in mind. One single goal. But one act almost destroyed all that. One act.

He pounded his fist down on the table. It was always something so minute that paved the way for consequences.

He'd show them. They thought to handicap him but they were mistaken. If there was one thing he'd learned throughout the ages, it was that trust was a dead man's noose.

Their handicap was his salvation. If only they knew they played right into his hands.

The air around him stilled while the growing rumble of a motorcycle grew louder. It was about time.

He pushed back his chair and went to stand on the front porch of the dilapidated cottage he'd kept over the years. It was surrounded by overgrown weeds and trees and only a handful knew its location.

"You'd better tell me you have him." His daughter pulled off her helmet and glared at him.

He would have laughed other than the fact she'd probably try to kill him if he did.

"I don't. But I know where he is."

Visible relief swept over her body, and not for the first time did he wonder if he did the right thing.

"Let's go then." She stood there, erect and demanding. It was laughable how the tables turned and how quickly. There was a time when she was afraid of him. It was evident that time was long gone.

Morax turned his back and headed towards his prison. The irony of it all. The broken boards, the tell-tale animal droppings, and that smell...

"Don't walk away from me," Eva called after him. He pulled out a chair and sat down, then kicked the chair across from him out from beyond the table and waited. He counted the seconds it took for her to leave her precious motorcycle and make her way inside.

"All right, Father," she said. "What is going on."

Morax leaned forward and rested his elbows on the table. "Did you not notice a shield around the area when you drove up?"

She shrugged. "I figured you reinforced security. What of it."

"And yet you drove through with such ease, didn't you?"

Eva leaned back in her chair and flicked her ponytail behind her. "I'm not in the mood for chit-chat, Morax. I need Nathan. I need him now."

"Tsk, tsk, little child. Your impatience may one day be your undoing." He drew his fingers along the grain of the table. "I can't go anywhere, at the moment. And even if I could, it wouldn't do either of us any good."

"What do you mean you can't go anywhere?"

Morax crossed his legs and glanced upward. "That shield out there wasn't my doing. I've been...how do you say it...disciplined? No one in and no one out. Meaning, me." He swore he heard laughter in the distance.

"But I got in."

He nodded. "Yes, yes you did. Amazing, that, isn't it?" A smile crept on his face as confusion swept over his daughter. She still didn't understand, still didn't see how she played into this. She would and when she did, all hell would break loose. Literally. And that was something he was counting on.

"What game are you playing now?" She crossed his arms and stared at him.

Morax held up his hands in mock surrender. "I assure you, this is no game. Things are..." he had to word things carefully, no doubt others were listening in, "progressing beyond my control, at the moment. Nathan has...turned..." he let his voice drop off.

"It's not my fault!"

No, it wasn't. But he couldn't let her know that. Not yet and especially not now. She had her own role to play in this, a role greater than he'd let on.

"I warned you what would happen if you weren't there to help him, to protect him."

Eva sank into the chair, her whole body bowed over in despair. "I failed him," she mumbled.

Morax leaned forward and placed his hand on her back. "Yes, you did." He watched as her shoulders dropped lower. She was no good to him like this. He needed her to be a warrior, his warrior. "But if you don't go after him, you'll also be the one responsible for his death," he whispered very softly into her ear.

Her head raised before he dug his fingers into her back, forcing her back down.

"It's all your fault," he said out loud. He could feel her muscles bunch beneath his hand. *Good girl.* "I didn't raise you for a fool and yet all you've done is mope after this boy like a love-sick little puppy. He was the answer. The one I needed. And you let him slip between our fingers like sand on a dry beach." He added a little extra venom to his voice.

Eva's head slowly raised and there was a little twinkle in her eye. "If you had helped me instead of handicapping me every step of the way, none of this would have happened. Don't be blaming me, *Father*," she spat out the title as if it was venom on her tongue, "for your own failures."

Morax pulled away. There was a small table with a single drawer. In that drawer was one small item. He reached inside and pulled it out.

"I need you to do something for me." He said as he cupped his hand to hide what was inside.

"Why would I do anything for you, especially now?" Eva stood, her long black hair over her shoulder, and glared.

"If you want to remain alive, you'll get rid of that petulant tone and not dare to cross me. Don't fool yourself. This," he waved his hands in the air, "if of little consequence." Being stuck here suited his purposes more than anyone would ever know.

"Why are you here anyway?"

Morax crossed the room and stood before his daughter. "Oh you know, I have a habit of not playing well with others. Seems I crossed a line somewhere along the way, and they decided it was time for me to pay the price."

He grabbed hold of Eva's hand and forced her fist to open. "Return this to its owner." He dropped the item into the palm of her hand.

"Who?" Her fingers closed around his gift.

"You'll figure that out. Eventually." He turned his back on her and sat back down at the table, his fingers drumming on the wood. "Go on now, there's not much time left."

"Who is making you pay?"

Morax sighed. "What happened to the days of the little girl obeying every word her father commanded?"

Eva laughed. "What does the term *Restorer* mean to you?"

Morax' body stilled as nervous anticipation coursed through his veins. "The Restorer is my salvation." He said quietly.

She must have heard him. Her footsteps echoed against the wood floors, and within moments, he felt the touch of her mind against his.

Then let me introduce myself.

CHAPTER
FORTY-THREE

NATHAN

Two days had passed since that day in the park and Nathan's world had changed forever. Keys dangled from Nathan's fingers as he sat in his truck and waited for Zeke to join him.

Too many days had passed and he was tired of hiding.

"Are you sure you're ready?" Zeke walked towards him carrying an old wooden chest in his arms.

"Honestly? I'm not sure of anything anymore, but I can't stay locked up here. I'm done running away. It's time to face my fears and Eva."

"Once the two of you are together, you'll be stronger." Zeke stowed the chest at the back of Nathan's truck and opened the passenger door.

"So you keep saying, and yet it was your decision to remain here, hidden for the past couple of days." He gunned the gas and drove down the long pebbled driveway that led away from the rustic cabin in the mountains that Zeke called home.

"I needed to ensure your safety."

Nathan only grunted. He was tired of hearing those same words over and over again.

Two days ago Zeke had whisked him away mere seconds before the black swirl above him covered him.

One minute, Nathan was surrounded by blackness, and then next, he was in the midst of a warming light that permeated every bone in his body and coursed through his veins with a power unlike anything he'd ever known.

"Why is my safety so important to you anyway?" Nathan glanced over at Zeke and caught the way the man's hands curled into a fist. "You call yourself a friend, but you seem to know more about me than you should."

"I once was a friend of your mother's. I made her a promise years ago to look out for you when the time came." The words were spoken soft like, with a hint of familiarity to them.

When the time came. What did Zeke mean by that?

"How did you know my mother?"

"We once had...a mutual acquaintance." The way Zeke said the words, Nathan knew there was a lot of history behind that sentence.

"Morax, you mean?"

Zeke nodded. "I met your mother shortly after she left Morax. I was there to help her understand, to get her through those dark days."

Understanding flowed through Nathan at that moment. He recalled a few sentences throughout his mother's journals talking about Zeke, her angel. At the time he'd figured she meant figuratively.

"So what do we do now?" He didn't even want to get into that conversation. They'd talked about his destiny until they were both exhausted over the past few days in that cabin. But they'd never discussed what would happen now. Now that he was a Nephilim.

"Now we try to keep you alive. Most Nephilim are killed before they turn."

"And those who aren't killed?" Nathan swallowed past the lump in his throat.

Zeke nodded. "There are few who do survive, but they don't live long."

"They're killed by the Guardians, aren't they?" Nathan tightened his fingers along the steering wheel.

"No. The Guardians are there to protect the Nephilim. A Nephilim can not survive without their Guardian, and won't when their protectors are killed." A weariness settled in Zeke's voice.

"Killed by whom?"

Zeke sighed and stared out the passenger window. Minutes of silence passed between them as they drove down a narrow road. It wasn't until they hit the highway that Zeke turned towards Nathan and spoke.

"The Guard. Brothers and sisters to the Guardians."

CHAPTER
FORTY-FOUR

EVA

It was dark by the time Eva made it back to Redemption. She didn't give her surroundings much thought as she wove her way down roads on her way to her house, but on her left as she passed through intersections, she caught a distinct glow.

She turned her bike down one of the streets and slowed down as she watched crowds of families and friends make their way along the sidewalks. They were all headed in the same direction. The town square.

The town was ablaze in lights once again. Shocked covered Eva's face as she parked her bike on the side and slowly got off. She couldn't believe it. Recently the large walnut tree that stood in the centre of the park had been uprooted and left a gaping hole in the ground. And yet tonight, there stood the mighty tree once again, soaring high up above their heads. Thousands of Christmas lights dangled beneath and amongst its branches, showering the park with light.

"Looks good, doesn't it?" Kate appeared beside Eva and crossed her arms, a happy smile on her face.

"It looks amazing. Almost like nothing had ever happened." Flowering bushes surrounded the park along with potted plants that lined the walkways.

"Oh, it happened all right," Kate glanced over at the burned remains of her cafe, "but this town is a sanctuary and that's what it will remain."

"How--"

Kate shook her head. "Don't ask, just enjoy."

Eva followed Kate as she made her way to the tree where Jack and another woman stood.

"You did good, Jack. Look at everyone arriving, you can see their happiness and peace." Kate linked arms with her husband as she stared out at the families were filled the town square.

"A little peace does the soul good. Now, time to get to work." Jack laid a small kiss on Kate's cheek before he headed towards his truck parked next to Eva's bike. She didn't even realize she'd parked beside him.

"Eva, this is Shelly, my sister. I don't think you've met."

Eva reached out to shake Shelly's hand and was surprised at the jolt of warmth she received when they touched.

"We have. Years ago." Shelly winked at her. "We bumped into each other at Nathan's wedding."

As Eva thought back, she vaguely recalled standing beside Shelly at the back of the church before Shelly went to sit down.

"Nice to meet you," Eva pulled her hand away and glanced up at the tree.

Restorer.

Eva smiled. She held out her arm and waited for Shadow to land there. She watched Shelly out of the corner of her eye to see if the woman would react but was surprised when the woman reached out and gently stroked the top of Shadow's head.

"I've always liked crows," she said.

Eva shrugged and then turned to Kate. "Please tell me you've heard from Nathan."

On the drive back from seeing Morax, Eva realized that everything had changed. Her whole life she'd been prepared to help Nathan through the change and had never really considered what would happen after that.

She knew if she wasn't there for him, he wouldn't survive, so that's all she'd focused on for years was ensuring she would be there, by his side, helping him.

Except, he'd already gone through the change, he'd already turned into a Nephilim and Eva wasn't sure what her role was anymore.

Restorer.

Eva shook her head at Shadow. *Not now.* She needed to figure out where Nathan was and what the next steps would be. Morax's last words to her hung over her head like a heavy fog clouding her judgment.

"You know nothing. If you really were the Restorer, you wouldn't be here, concerned about Nathan. You wouldn't need that boy anymore."

Was she really the protector like everyone was calling her?

"I was hoping you had." Kate shook her head but glanced over at Shelly with an odd look on her face.

"What aren't you telling me?" Eva demanded to know. She was tired of all the secrets. Tired of all the games people assumed she knew how to play.

"I saw him a few days ago. We were...attacked...and he disappeared before I could make sure he was all right." Shelly hedged.

"He wasn't your responsibility." Kate folded her arms over her chest and frowned.

"What do you mean you were attacked and he disappeared? And why didn't you help him?" Anger, rage, and disbelief all flowed through Eva, and her hands bunched in a fist. Shadow flew off her arm and circled the air above her.

Calm Restorer. Calm.

Thunder boomed across the sky and the startled shrieks of the children filled the air.

"That's enough, girl. Reign in those emotions of yours before I do it for you." Jack walked up behind her with a canister dangling off one arm and a bunch of styrofoam cups in his hand.

He grabbed one, filled it with hot chocolate from the canister, and handed it to Eva.

Eva pursed her lips but didn't say anything. She held the hot cup in her hands and glared at the women beside her. "I need explanations, Kate." She said.

"You don't need nothing. Shelly's not responsible for Nathan. You were. Someone took over your job. Enough said. The boy will be fine. He'll come when it's time." Jack handed Kate and Shelly both a cup of hot liquid before he ambled off to a family huddled together glancing up at the tree.

Someone took over? What?

"What has Morax told you about Zeke?" Kate asked.

"Nothing." But he would, the next time she saw him. She'd make sure of that.

"Zeke is his brother. A Guardian. Nathan's Guardian. He's been in hiding for the last little while. We've all done what we could to protect that boy of ours, and ensuring nothing happened to Zeke was part of that." Shelly explained.

"And yet, he's always been around," Kate muttered.

Shelly nodded. "He pops up every so often. I caught sight of him with Nathan before we were attacked. Joanne...his mother was hurt, so my focus was on her. I trusted Zeke to protect Nathan, and I'm sure that's what he's done."

No. Not good enough. Eva forced a long, slow breath out of her lungs.

Restorer. Attention.

Eva focused on Shadow who hovered in the air above her, gliding in a large circle around the tree.

I am paying attention. What am I missing?

Just then, a sharp pain pierced through Eva's brain and she clutched her head. It felt as if something tight had attached itself to her and pulled. Lights danced about her as she turned around in circles, trying to pinpoint where the pain was coming from. She caught the faint buzz of a familiar feeling and almost fell to her knees.

"He's back," she whispered as she reached out for something to steady her. Kate grabbed onto her hands and pulled her close, encircling her with her arms.

"You feel him? Where is he?" Kate's voice broke as she stroked Eva's back in a motherly fashion. Eva pulled away and wanted to run to her bike. Everything inside of her told her to go find him, to ensure he was okay.

Wait.

Shadow landed on her shoulder and pecked at her cheek. Eva moved her head but didn't say anything. She relished in the feel of Nathan's presence in her mind. She'd missed him. She'd missed this feeling.

Where are you? She didn't expect him to answer. She knew he wouldn't hear her. Not yet. But she still called out to him.

Here. His voice whispered across her mind like a smooth caramel as it melted on the tongue.

"Where is he?" Kate clutched at her arm.

"He's coming," Eva whispered. A smile settled over her face as she stepped away from the women, the tree, and all the people gathered in the park. She walked towards the far corner as if in a daze.

She ignored all the strange looks she received and only focused on the strange strand of light that illuminated the way before her. She'd never seen anything like that light before.

It led out of the park and down the street, but she stopped once she reached the sidewalk. She knew where the light led to. Whom it led to.

I'm coming. Nathan's voice whispered. A warmth spread throughout her body at the sound of his voice and an insurgence of energy whisked through her. She'd never felt so awake, so on fire as she did right now.

Flashes of light lit up the sky above her. She half expected the wind to pick up, for a storm to manifest itself as Nathan drew closer, but it didn't.

Bright lights came around the corner and Eva knew it was Nathan's truck.

Her heart leaped, and she felt like a schoolgirl about to head to the prom. What was wrong with her?

When Nathan pulled up and stepped out of his truck, Eva launched herself at him, not caring about how it looked. All she knew was that she needed to be in his arms, to know for sure that he was okay.

The moment his arms encircled her and he held her close, tears ran down her cheeks as she clung to him. He was different. He felt different. His body was harder, more solid, and defined. Not only that, but his essence had changed. Gone was the soft and uncertain man she'd always known. Instead, when she gazed up into his eyes, she found a man who was sure of himself, who knew his destiny.

A Nephilim.

"Oh God, Eva. I've missed you." He whispered.

Eva just clung to him, uncaring about what going on around them. She ignored the screams and the shouts.

The world could fall apart for all she cared. Nathan was back and she felt whole.

He was her world.

CHAPTER
FORTY-FIVE

NATHAN

Nathan couldn't believe what he saw as he held Eva in his arms. He wanted to block it all out and just enjoy the feel of this woman, *his woman* in his arms, but he couldn't.

The first thing he noticed was the tree. It was back, upright, as if it had never been pulled from its roots and tossed around like a flimsy branch in an autumn wind. Groups of people were milled around the tree, completely oblivious to the *other* beings winding their way around the people.

He had no idea what they were, but he knew they weren't supposed to be there.

"That's the cacodaemon you're seeing." Zeke stepped out from the truck and stood beside him.

Nathan shook his head as Eva stepped out of his arms. "The what?"

Eva turned. "I've never seen so many in one place."

Nathan placed his arm around her as she leaned into him.

"Thank you for protecting him and helping him when I couldn't." Eva said to Zeke.

"It was never your job. That's where Morax mislead you." Zeke reached over and placed his hand on her arm. A similar reaction to what she'd felt when she'd touched Shelly happened with his touch.

"I'm not sure what to believe anymore."

Zeke stepped forward and faced them. "No, you both know what you believe. It's at the very core of who you are. Separate, you are nothing. Together, you may be the salvation of a race doomed to eternal damnation. You're their hope."

A loud caw filled the air as a murder of crows swarmed above them. Nathan grimaced. He still didn't like the vile creatures no matter what Eva or Zeke said.

We are not the enemy, son of Morax.

A shiver ran down his spine at the words. Who was the enemy? Once upon the time, he would have assumed the heavenly guard were there to protect him. Now he finds out they are out to kill him.

Was he doomed, just like the Fallen?

"You have a choice. You've always had a choice." Zeke whispered beside him.

It was all they'd spoken about on their way here. Nathan's soul and what it meant to be Nephilim - the son of a Fallen angel. Was he an abomination in the sight of God?

Eva linked her fingers with his and pulled him forward.

"There are people here who need to see you." They wove their way around the dark beings, the cacodaemons who all bowed as they passed by, until they stood in front of Jack and Kate who waited for them.

"You've got quite the entourage there, boy." Jack stood there, with his feet planted apart and crossed his arms over his massive chest.

Nathan copied Jack's stance and stared down at the man before he couldn't keep the grin in any longer and leaned forward to wrap his arms around Jack's body.

"I've missed you too," Nathan said.

Jack patted his back. "Don't worry, your mother is safe."

Nathan sighed in relief, ignoring the obvious that Jack shouldn't have known about his mother to begin with before he stepped away and found himself engulfed in Kate's embrace. She squeezed him tight while patting his back. There were tears in her eyes as she looked him over.

"I'm okay, Kate." He tried to reassure her. He wasn't used to seeing her like this and it made him uncomfortable.

"I know you are," she said before she stepped away and composed herself.

Nathan pulled Eva close to him and looked around. "As good as new, huh?"

"You certainly are." Eva squeezed his arm and smiled at him.

Thunder rumbled again and the flashes of lightening lit up the sky with flashes of color.

"That's not me," Eva said to Jack.

Jack's lips thinned. "I know girl. I know."

"What is going on?" Nathan asked. He looked to Jack, then Kate and finally over to Zeke who stood behind him.

"It's time." Another voice answered and he turned to find Sheriff Bryant, coming towards him.

"He's not ready, Cam. It can't be." Eva shook her head.

"Will someone please tell me what is going on?" Nathan's body hummed from energy that surrounded him. Everyone but Eva stepped back from him.

"He doesn't need to be ready. You do." Cam pulled his hat off and glanced up at the sky. "I'm not liking the look of this. We should get everyone out of the way."

Jack shook his head. "And go where exactly? If this is what we think it is, it won't matter."

"What is it?" Nathan all but yelled.

His body warmed and his breathing quickened as dark clouds whirled above him. He could see a tiny opening in the middle of them, a small speck of a brilliant light. As he stared at that opening, a strange sense of peace flooded him and in an instant he knew.

He knew.

"This isn't our fight," he said to Eva.

She shook her head. "Of course it is. This is what we were created for. This is what it means to be a Nephilim. We're the bridge."

"No." Nathan dropped Eva's hand and turned in a circle, taking in everyone around him. The dark beings, the cacodaemons all watched him as if waiting to see what he would do, how he would react.

Everyone waited for him to react, but he wasn't going to. That's not what this was about.

Yes, he'd remembered what he'd read in his mother's journal, and he'd listened as Zeke told him the story of when that one decision made at the beginning of time changed the world for the angels or the fallen angels, and he knew that everyone expected him to do something about that. But he wasn't going to.

It wasn't up to him. He wasn't sure how he knew that, but he did.

The opening above him enlarged until it was the size of his fist and then his head.

"Together, we can change history," Eva said beside him. "Together, we can right a wrong."

Nathan reached out and grabbed hold of Eva's shoulders, pulling her close. "This isn't our wrong to right."

"I don't understand. Of course, it is. This is why we were created. This is what Morax has worked so long for - to right his wrong." Confusion covered Eva's face as she searched his eyes.

"Morax didn't create us. God did. Just like he created the Guardians and the Fallen." He glanced over his shoulder and found Jack smiling at him. "We all have a choice. They made their choice knowing what the consequences would be. But their choice wasn't ours. It isn't ours. We have our own path and it's not to ease a regret."

He glanced up and was amazed at what he saw beyond the dark clouds and the brilliant light that now shone down on both him and Eva. He looked to Jack and to Zeke to see if they saw the same thing and realized that the dark beings that had filled the park were gone, and everyone in the park was no longer standing.

All but him and Eva had bowed their knees as their gazes were lifted high.

This is what he'd been created for. Light filled his being as a gentle wind surrounded him. He slowly released Eva, took her hand, and pulled her to the ground with him as he bent his own knee.

In surrender.

CHAPTER
FORTY-SIX

MORAX

Morax stood motionless in the cold, sparse room, visions of what was happening played out before him.

He'd been wrong.

Deep agony filled him as he realized everything he'd been working for had been for nothing.

Nothing could save him now.

A chill settled over him as he viewed the hell that was now his home. The scorched cement blocks reminded him of his own soul, forever burned, their scars always there.

The fingers of long-ago flames licked the walls and left burn patterns snaking toward the ceiling. The little cracks in the floor crisscrossed each other until the kaleidoscope of weeds peeping through the cracks decorated the floor. Ants and other insects covered his boots as he stood there.

After centuries of holding onto a hope of redemption, he now understood the truth. He'd lived a lie, one of his own making. He'd been warned, along with his other brothers that their fate was sealed. Who was he to attempt to right a wrong?

Who was he to once again attempt to be like his own creator? Like God?

The slight swoosh of wings alerted him to a presence and he turned to find a crow standing on the table behind him.

Eva's crow. Shadow.

Something flashed in his beak. Morax stepped closer and knew right away what it was. It was the one thing he'd given Eva the last time he saw her.

A fish scale.

Not within her power to undo your wrong.

Morax pulled out a chair and sat down. "She could have, if she'd tried."

Some wrongs cannot be unmade.

"Tell me you don't wish things to be different. Don't you miss the feel of the rushing water against your scaly body?"

Living in the past destroys the present.

Morax waved his hand in the air. He didn't need the crow to preach to him. There had to be a way to undo this, to heal Joanne, to fix his mistake.

Even if it took another millennium, he would find a way. He would not, could not accept that a lesser being than himself was more favored by God.

It may be the last and only thing he'll ever do, but he will find his own redemption.

The End

MORE BOOKS COMING YOUR WAY

If you're waiting for the next Asylum Confession book, it's coming your way.

What else can you expect from me?

My VIP ADDICTS subscription group knows...I've got a haunted house series that I'm working on, if you're interested in that.

https://reamstories.com/jacksteen

CONFESSION BOOK #1

The Asylum Confessions

They arrive alive. They always leave dead. But first, they give me their confessions.

This is the one that started it all! These are a few of my favorite confessions - if you haven't already read them, I hope you enjoy the journey!